MURDER FOR A RAINY DAY

Murder for a Rainy Day

Pecan Bayou, Volume 6

Teresa Trent

Published by Teresa Trent, 2014.

This is a work of fiction. Similarities to real people, places, or events are entirely coincidental.

MURDER FOR A RAINY DAY

First edition. October 22, 2014.

ISBN: 978-1732946859

Written by Teresa Trent.

Acknowledgements

I would like to thank Pat Cegan for sharing her poem, *Dreams*. I would also like to thank MSgt Brian J. Lamar from the Air Force Reserve 53rd Weather Reconnaissance Squadron or the "Hurricane Hunters" for his valuable information.

Finally, I would like to thank my editor, Diane Krause. Your attention to detail is amazing. Thanks for helping me to be a better writer.

Dedication

To my dad. I will always treasure our time together.

CHAPTER 1

Dreams

What are dreams?
Do they hold some mystical
message? Are they wrappings
for lessons we need to learn?
Prophesies? Warnings, promises?
How concealed is all, yet at
the same time, transparently
clear. The veil is lifting. We
are awakening again and again.
As layers are peeled away, how
wonder-filled life is.
~Pat Cegan

"Well it's official," my father said. "We now have the most lame-ass town entrance in the whole state of Texas."

Scowling, he dropped the freshly severed hand of cowboy star Charlie Loper to the ground. It landed with a thud.

"Offensive my ass. That was Charlie Loper's signature pose. The man is nothing without his six shooter. Now he looks like the butterfly whisperer."

I have to admit my father was right.

Although Charlie Loper had been dead for more than fifty years, he was immortalized in bronze thirty years ago and has been ushering visitors into Pecan Bayou ever since. Pecan Bayou, Texas held bragging rights to only two things: growing the biggest and best pecans in the state of Texas, and being the boyhood home of matinee idol Charlie Loper. His daughter, Libby Loper, still lived in Pecan Bayou and kept Charlie's memory alive through the Charlie Loper Deadeye Museum and a newly-opened dude ranch.

And now, bronze Charlie Loper had been neutralized. The hand holding his six shooter was gone, a new one being welded into place. The cowboy's new pose did indeed look as if he as if he would never dream of using a gun.

My dad's clenched fist rested on the revolver tucked comfortably on his hip—standard issue for the Pecan Bayou Police Department. I wondered if he was aware of the grip he held on his own gun while he watched Charlie Loper's being sliced away.

Even if the non-violent Charlie were alive and standing here today, there would be no butterflies fluttering about. Mosquitoes were the only insects that could tolerate temperatures in the high 90s, with humidity that registered somewhere between a sauna and the steam from a pot of boiling water.

Today was a big day for my father, so it was important for me to be here, but this environment was brutal for a woman who's nine months pregnant. I had just come from my weekly appointment with Dr. Randall, my obstetrician, who said she'd be surprised if this baby stays put longer than two weeks.

Sweat trickled down from my hairline and I felt like I was wrapped in a blanket. Normally, my caring and attentive father would have been fussing over me, but the disarming of Charlie Loper – the hero of my father's youth – had him completely unsettled. I just hoped I wouldn't pass out before this whole thing was over.

As a welder attached two thin metal strips to Charlie's shiny new outstretched hand, a pickup truck approached, pulling the likeness of Charlie Loper's famous horse, Ol' Bess. She'd just made the two-mile journey from the Charlie Loper Deadeye Museum to join Charlie at the corner of Main and Pecan.

For the most part, Pecan Bayou is a quiet little town with just a few restaurants, a movie theater, churches, schools, a library, and a public pool. The streets are filled with families who have lived here all their lives. We're a small spot on the map, but not really that different from any other city or town with gossip, marriages and divorces, new babies and sad goodbyes.

My father, Judd Kelsey, was a lieutenant on the Pecan Bayou Police Force, and although a heavy day of crime might involve a lost dog and a dispute over the bingo money over at the church, he still had strong opinions on the right to bear arms.

Now, a more peaceful Charlie Loper would greet all who entered our quaint little town.

As I watched two strapping guys unload Ol' Bess, I was certain my father was right. The cowboy statue and his newly added horse were a strange couple. While Charlie was made of bronze, wearing a classic weathered patina, the horse looked like it was plucked directly from Ronald McDonald's play yard. Leave it to Pecan Bayou to take its best cash cow and screw it up. Now this mismatched pair would stand at the main roadway into town, greeting our visitors and giving them a glimpse of how looney we all are.

I reached into my purse for the Gatorade that I had been carrying around. I swallowed, but choked as the green liquid hit the back of my throat. The drink had been cool just a few minutes before, but now it felt warm and sour. As I gasped for breath, my father finally turned around and looked at me.

"Oh darlin'. Do you really think you ought to be standing out here in the heat?"

"I'm fine," I lied.

During my first pregnancy, I had been an attractive pregnant woman. Well, as attractive as one can be with an extra thirty-five pounds. But the extra weight had been in the front, where it should be. This time around, I put on weight in the front, the back, on the top and on the bottom. And the pounds kept piling on. I was only a few weeks from delivery, and at this point, I was counting down the hours.

To make matters worse, my husband Leo, a meteorologist, was kicking into high gear as hurricane season got into full swing. This summer had been abnormally hot, and the waters in the Gulf were starting to heat up.

The recipe for a hurricane is simple. Take a storm off the coast of Africa and let it drift across to the United States. Trap the storm the warm waters of the Gulf of Mexico and let it churn. The more it churns, the bigger it gets.

For as long as I can remember, Pecan Bayou and other towns north of Houston have played happy hosts to evacuees wielding credit cards, looking for places to escape the wind and rain. The only problem though, was that often these hurricanes made landfall and triggered other storm events like tornadoes.

I occasionally wondered if people up north scratch their heads and ask themselves why anyone would live in a hurricane zone. All I can say is sometimes you're born in a place and that is where you stay. It takes more than swirling clouds and record-breaking heat to run us out.

Even if we do have the most lame-ass entrance of any town in Texas.

Welcome to Pecan Bayou.

CHAPTER 2

Once the new Charlie Loper and his trusty horse were settled in, the crowd dispersed and went home. When I walked in the house, I was welcomed by a cool blast of air conditioning and Butch, our over-exuberant Weimeraner. Butch followed faithfully as I headed to the kitchen for a large glass of cold water.

"Hey boy." I patted the eighty-pound monstrosity we called a dog on the head and received a slobbery lick in return.

As I set down my glass and reached for a towel, I once again failed to account for my protruding belly and knocked a cherub-faced pink piggy bank right off the counter. The little pig hit the ground, breaking into four parts. Not only was I startled by the crash, but a pang of guilt hit me, as this had been a gift for the baby from my husband's mother, Gwyn.

After recovering from a momentary fright, Butch began prancing around, contaminating the crime scene. I grabbed his collar and gently tugged him toward the back door.

"Come on boy. Let's put you in the yard for a few minutes." He happily bounded out into the yard and set about looking for something to pee on.

Closing the door, I returned to the broken pig and squatted down to pick up the remains. As I picked up the largest intact chunk, a shiny silver dollar went rolling under the refrigerator. Another pang of guilt.

The pig's head was still attached to its body, and wrapped around its neck was a yellow ribbon holding a small card that read "Sus domesticus for our newest homo sapien." Yes, it was a strange sentiment, but not out of character for my new mother-in-law, Gwyn Fitzpatrick, who was a biology teacher. It was sweet sentiment, in an obsessively scientific labeling sort of way.

I needed to rescue the pig if at all possible. Gwyn lived in Galveston, so she visited often and would be certain to notice if the piggy bank were missing from the baby's nursery.

Maybe I could glue it back together again and no one would even notice. I spread the shattered pieces of porcelain out on the counter. There was one break around the back and one on the leg. One ear was broken and the curly tail had popped off. The body itself was still intact.

I stepped into my office to find my notebooks, alphabetized by topic. These books were my primary resource for writing my helpful hints column. I quickly located a section on gluing and learned I needed some sort of epoxy adhesive to mend the broken pig properly.

Returning to the kitchen, I began digging through the glue stash in the utility cabinet. All I could find was an old bottle of school glue leftover from one of the boy's discarded school supplies. Not epoxy, but worth a shot.

I grabbed yesterday's paper from the recycling bin and spread it out on the counter. I had already made one mess; I certainly didn't want to be scraping glue off my marble countertops later.

Arranging the pig remnants, I looked down to see the face of Tom Schuller smiling up at me from the newspaper. The headline announced Tom was leaving his long-term post on the Pecan Bayou City Council.

Tom served on city council alongside his brother Don, and the two of them had ruled these positions for many years. Tom owned Schuller Auto and Don ran the Pecan Bayou Chamber of Commerce. You could hardly walk a block in this town without running into a smiling Schuller ready to make a deal.

Schuller Auto was one of the most successful businesses in town, so it came as a shock to many in Pecan Bayou when Tom and his wife announced they were giving the dealership to their son, and planned to travel across America in a thirty-nine foot RV. Not that there were that many controversial decisions to make in city council, but most residents agreed Don Schuller would miss his brother's duplicate vote.

I opened the bottle and ran a line of glue on the tail, then carefully positioned it on the pig's backside. After a minute, I loosened my grip on the tail. It fell off. This wasn't going to work. I would have to buy a tube of epoxy and try again later. I just had to hope I could get the little pig put back together before Leo's mother visited. She would be driving up from Galveston for the birth of the baby and I needed to be sure the pig had plenty of time to dry before then.

As I put away the glue, I felt the baby inside me stretch. It wouldn't be long now, and this little one was becoming extremely active. I rested my hand on the baby wondering if I was touching his head or the other end. Sometimes it felt like my unborn child was doing jumping jacks inside. I couldn't wait to meet this new person who would be such a wonderful part of our world. The phone was ringing as I stepped back into the kitchen.

"Mom?" My son Zach was on the other end of the line.

" Hi Zach. I was wondering when you would call."

"Yeah, Mom. Listen..."

I wasn't sure if I liked the way this conversation was starting. I could tell he probably had friends standing behind him at the summer camp he was attending. It had been a tough decision for us to send my twelve-year-old son Zach, and Leo's thirteen-year-old son Tyler, to summer camp. With the baby coming, we decided the boys going to camp would simplify our lives and give us the opportunity to focus on the delivery. The boys wanted to go with their friends anyway, so the two of them were in North Texas enjoying a month-long scout camp. I expected daily calls complaining of homesickness, but instead they called weekly because the counselor made them. So much for missing us.

"Mom, are you still there?"

"Yes I'm here. How are you doing?"

"Oh, I'm fine. I just wanted to ask you... because I know you'd be concerned for our well-being... it seems we may have run a little short on funds up here."

Wasn't he a little young to be already calling his mother for money?

"How can you be running short? Your dad and I sent plenty of money to last you the entire month."

"I know. But here's the thing..." I closed my eyes as Zach launched into his explanation, while his sibling was starting to do somersaults in the womb.

"...so you see we had no idea that they meant real money in the card game?"

I sighed.

"Funny, huh?" Zach laughed, trying to get me to see the humor in the situation.

"Let me speak to your camp counselor."

"Now, Mom. You don't have to go all nuclear on me. It was a simple mistake. The only problem is Tyler and I don't have any money now. We really do need those sports drinks after a long day on the trail."

"Let me talk to your counselor."

"What's that?" Zach said, his voice focused away from the phone. "Gee, Mom I have to go now. Don't forget to send the money." There was a click on the other end. Unbelievable.

I speed-dialed Leo. If I had to guess who got Zach in a poker game, my money would be on Leo's son. Not to say that my son was more innocent than Tyler, but Tyler was much more of a risk taker.

"Hey, Betsy. I'm so glad you called," Leo said. Even though he said he was glad to hear from me, he sounded distracted. Nothing like working in the weather bureau in August.

"Actually, I hadn't planned on calling you but..."

"Still, I needed to talk to you. We're beginning to get some movement in the Gulf. You know we've been watching these storms coming across the Atlantic. They're really starting to build. Models are indicating the next few weeks could be pretty interesting."

I wondered if Leo was aware he was using his network weatherman voice. After his experience nine months ago filling in for our local weather guru Hurricane Hal, parts of his on-air voice never left him. In reality he hated being a television weatherman, but the experience left some lasting impressions on him.

"That's great to know, Leo, but pretty predictable for Texas in summer time."

"Yes, yes I know. You're right, but this is very exciting."

"Did you know your sons are gambling at scout camp?" I hated to be rude, but I knew we were about to move to cloud patterns and swirling winds. Leo's weather predictions stalled on the other end. I had achieved the effect that I was going for.

"They're what?"

"Gambling. Zach just called and asked for us to float some money his way. He said he didn't know they were playing for real money."

"Oh, this will never do. This is one of those times when I really wish the camp would let the boys carry their own cell phones. I can't believe that they would allow him to play for money."

I hadn't missed Leo was speaking only of Zach. How did he know that Tyler hadn't been involved in the game, too?

"I tried to get him to put the scout leader on the line and Zach hung up on me."

"He hung up? You mean he hung up on his own mother after asking for money? "

"Pretty much."

"Do you think we should bring the boys home? Maybe this scout camp wasn't such a good idea. I don't remember seeing any poker tables in the brochure."

"I don't know, Leo."

"We could have my mom come up early. She could watch Zach and Tyler while we are busy at the hospital."

I stopped for a moment to consider this idea. The boys were old enough, they wouldn't be too much work. It would work, but somehow I just felt better with our original plan. I hated to ask Gwyn to change her plans.

"No, I don't want to put your mom to all that trouble."

"No trouble at all. She'll be here for the baby anyway."

"I know. Let me think about this for a little bit." I heard someone call to Leo in the background.

"Betsy? I have to go now."

"Sure."

After making sure the pig was stable, I headed over to the town's only newspaper, the Pecan Bayou Gazette. I needed to talk to Rocky, the editor and my boss. I write a weekly helpful hints column for the Gazette titled *The Happy Hinter*. Rocky had emailed earlier telling me to come by to discuss a special assignment. Heaven knows what that would be.

When I trudged out of the heat into the Gazette office, Rocky was leaned back in his desk chair relishing in its annoying squeak.

"Well now, if it isn't little Miss Ready to Pop." Rocky's hair had been salt-and-pepper ever since I'd known him, and now it was turning to a silky shade of white. Still though, he had a full head of it which made him an object of desire among the town's population of single women over fifty. He never got serious with any of the well-wishing casserole carriers—probably the result of three failed marriages—but he did appreciate the free food.

Rocky's son, Nicholas, a modern version of his father, was busy tapping away at a computer when I entered the Gazette office. Nicholas had Rocky's good looks and did a heck of a job staying on top of the news. When Nicholas came into the family business he brought modern technology to a ticker tape newspaper office. Nicholas looked up briefly and nodded, never missing a keystroke.

I wasn't surprised to see my father, Judd Kelsey, leaning against a wall with his arms crossed. This was a familiar tableau, repeated over decades. The friendship between Rocky and my dad was a true love-hate relationship. They were old fishing buddies and from the same generation, but on opposite sides of the political spectrum. When it came to the local crime scene they were adversaries—my dad, a lifelong policeman, was out to arrest the bad guy, and Rocky was out to get in my dad's way covering the story. After Rocky's near brush with death last year, the two men, realizing time is precious, had grown even closer.

"Have a seat, Betsy. You look hot. I was just finishing up with ol' Clark Kent here."

My dad pulled out a chair for me and then turned back to Rocky. "So, you haven't heard anything at all about the guy?"

I gently lowered myself down into the chair feeling like a hot air balloon coming in for a landing.

"Not a thing," Rocky answered. "I didn't even know he was missing. Sad about him losing his wife and all. Maybe it had something to do with that. Have you checked with his mother-in-law? Is she still around?"

"In the nursing home. I don't think she'd be much help," Judd said.

Rocky scratched his head. "I thought he was retiring. What about his kids?"

Judd nodded. "They all live out of state now and none of them have heard from him."

"Maybe he got in his car to drive off into the sunset and forgot to charge his cell phone."

"You're probably right. I'm just following up for one of his old poker buddies. He probably owes him money."

"I think we all have someone out there like that," Rocky said. My father pushed himself off the wall and turned towards me.

"How are you feeling today darlin'?"

"I'm hot, but I guess I'll survive." Though the thermometer outside read 96, it felt like more than 100. Dogs that normally ran around lay panting in the cool grass. The ice cream truck kept running out of Nutty Buddies and the local pool was overflowing with splashing children.

I shifted my gaze to Rocky. "So, you have a big assignment for me?"

"I had myself an epiphany of inspiration, and you are the woman for the job. I want to put you on it." I began to wonder if Rocky realized I would be taking some time off for the baby.

"An epiphany of inspiration? Isn't that redundant?" Nicholas looked up from his keyboard, one eyebrow raised.

"Your daddy is the media," my father told Nicholas. "Redundancy is his business."

Rocky scowled at him and then turned his attention back to me. "I suppose you've heard about the open seat on the city council?"

"I saw it in the paper."

"It's a true blessing to our readership. Here we are in the middle of a dull and boring news season, and we fall upon a closely contested city council race. If we're lucky, there'll be some mudslinging going on."

"And somehow this involves me?" I asked, my hand resting on my now moving belly.

"Why yes, it does, my Happy Hinter. We're going to have ourselves a political grill-off. Everybody knows that you can really judge a man by how he grills, and what he grills. It's a perfect combination of summertime tradition and hard-hitting politics."

"So, you want me to grill the candidates on grilling?" I asked. My father let out a laugh.

"Yes!" Rocky replied. "Get everything you can—secret recipes, as well as any grilling techniques you can pry out of them. Emphasize that this is their opportunity to serve their future constituents. Why, this could be the decision-maker for the voters of Pecan Bayou. I can't think of a more perfect way to rate our candidates. I mean seriously, would you vote for a man who chooses to grill some sort of namby-pamby health conscious chicken? Or would you vote for a man who will grill up a beefy ribeye and not give a hoot about that nasty ol' cholesterol?"

I was pretty sure the heat had infiltrated Rocky's thought processes.

"I don't know Rocky. I planned on wrapping up the column for a couple of months..."

"I know. You're having a baby. Just this one last writing assignment before you go. Once you have the recipes, you could knock it out in ten minutes. Just email that sucker over here to me at the Gazette and you can go off and put your feet in the stirrups and have that baby." Such a polite thing to say.

"I think it's a great idea," my father chimed in, even though nobody asked his opinion. Of course, that never stopped him before.

"What do you think, Nicholas?" Rocky asked.

Nicholas kept typing, his gaze never leaving the screen. "Huh?" Clearly, Nicholas was no longer part of the conversation.

I sighed, picked up a file off the desk next to me and started fanning myself. Why did it feel like the heat was on wherever I went?

"Come on Betsy. It'll help get your mind off the baby," Rocky said. As if that could happen.

I rolled my eyes and then gave in. "Okay, okay I'll do it, but then that's it. I am on maternity leave."

I slapped down the file and pulled myself up out of the chair. I wobbled slightly and felt Rocky and my dad's hands at my elbows. I shook them off. "I'm fine." They let go and stepped back out of hitting range. "So who are the two candidates?"

"The first man to put his hat in the ring is the one and only Baxter Digby," Rocky offered. Baxter Digby was one of Pecan Bayou's most successful real estate agents. Half the houses on our pecan tree lined streets had been sold by him. His smiling face was on so many front yard signs that small children could recognize him in the supermarket.

Somehow, the man always struck me as being just a little too good-looking. I also suspected he'd had a dentist add a couple of extra teeth to his blindingly white smile. I'd seen him standing outside the groundbreaking ceremony for the new hospital, and though there was a heavy wind, his hair didn't move an inch. Ruby Green, our local beautician and purveyor of beauty, he was wearing a wig.

She was probably right. His hair was too perfect.

Rocky continued. "Then our other contender is Drummond Struthers, the town tow truck driver and president of Pastor Green's congregation. This right here is what I hate to see happen. An honest man going into politics. They'll have him shape-changing within the hour."

Drummond's entry into the race was a surprise. He had never struck me as the political type, but you just never knew. Most of the low-income families in town appreciated his kindness. Drummond Struthers typically offered a special discounted rate for the broken down jalopies he was always towing for them. He genuinely cared for his fellow man, but the idea of asking a glorified mechanic for a grilling recipe might not be such a good one.

"So that's all there is to it Betsy. I just know you can make this sing for us. Once you get this little set of interviews done, just feel free to have yourself a baby. Have I mentioned what a good name Rocky is?"

"Yes. I believe you have."

"If it's a boy, you can name him Rocky, and if it's a girl, you can name her Rockette." He grinned, pleased with himself.

"Now you're sure you're okay with me taking some time off for the baby?"

"Not only am I okay with it, I'm looking forward to it," Rocky said. "You've been doing so much nesting around here, it's driving us all crazy. Who said you could put curtains in my bathroom?"

"You have to admit it looks a lot better now."

"I like them," Nicholas said.

"Besides, every time I used the restroom I worried somebody walking down the alley might be looking in the window at me. You need to think about the women in your life, Rocky."

"Something I try not to do too often. It tends to lead to alimony checks."

CHAPTER 3

"May I help you?" The receptionist asked. She sat behind a glass-topped desk held up by a curved steel frame. I waddled up to the waiting area. The rush of the air conditioner hitting my body caused me to stop for a moment. I took a breath and regained my composure. The woman's eyes widened as if she were afraid I was going to go into labor right there on the polished marble floor.

"I need to see Baxter Digby." Her look of astonishment continued as she noted my hand resting on my protruding belly. She gulped.

"Oh no! I'm from the Pecan Bayou Gazette and I just need to get a recipe from him for a feature we're doing on the candidates."

"Of course," she smiled, unable to hide her relief. She picked up the phone and punched in a number. "Someone from the paper is here to see you, Mr. Digby." She listened and then set down the phone. "Mr. Digby will be with you in just a moment."

I glanced over at a picture of Digby with his wife and two children. "That's Mr. Digby's family?"

"Oh yes. That's Dana Digby. She's wonderful. She studied nursing of some type, but when she had the children, decided she would be better at home raising them. I really admire her for deciding to do that. When is your baby due?"

"In a couple of weeks."

"Do you know if it's a boy or a girl?"

"Yes."

A hand reached out from nowhere. "Baxter Digby at your service." Digby squeezed my hand while pumping my arm up and down.

"Uh. Nice to meet you. I'm Betsy Fitzpatrick. I'm writing a piece on you and Drummond Struthers for the paper."

"Well, this is excellent, just excellent. I really admire how your paper has jumped in to give the candidates a voice. If we can't get our platforms out there on community issues then the people have no idea who to vote for. Today I just have to say — God bless America and its media outlets."

"Actually...."

"No, you should be commended. What should I start with? City planning? Zoning? My vision for a bright economic future?"

"Actually, I need a recipe."

"Pardon?"

"A recipe. I write the Happy Hinter column, and Rocky thought it might be good to have sort of an electoral grill-off."

His lips thinned. "I see."

"Are you an active griller?"

Baxter Digby straightened the flag pen on his lapel and stepped back. "Leave your card with my secretary, and I'll have my wife call you."

The freshly pressed back pleat of his navy sport coat swayed slightly in the breeze he created turning from me in a dash for the door.

"Thanks for your time, and I'm sure your simple recipe will go over well with the comments Drummond Struthers included with his grilling secrets. Who knew the guy knew so much about barbecue, and for that fact, life?"

Digby's head pivoted back toward me. He replaced his look of boredom with one of great interest.

"He gave you commentary? He shared wisdom? Folksy stuff?"

"Yes sir," I lied. I hadn't even spoken to Drummond Struthers yet. "This is America after all." Land of the free and home of an abundance of hot air, I thought.

"Well, then," he pushed the knot in his tie up. "I would be pleased to share my take on grilling and American life. It's just the kind of guy I am."

An hour later I sat with Drummond Struthers in the office of his automotive repair shop. He had the proud distinction of being the only tow truck driver in Pecan Bayou. When Struthers was not fixing or towing cars, he was the congregational president at Pastor Green's church. Drummond helped the church not only as a member of the church council, but had a hand in programs for the poor. Baxter Digby had given me such a good response when he found out his opponent contributed, I decided to let Drummond Struthers look through my notes. He glanced at my yellow legal pad full of scribbles. "So, you say Digby gave you all that?"

Digby had called home for a recipe and then expounded on the values of family life and the American way for at least five pages. Knowing that Rocky had a word limit, I wondered if he realized I would be using only about a tenth of what he was saying. Still though, it gave us good material to put in the paper.

"Yes. He shared so much good advice about grilling and really, life in general."

"I see." He said quietly. "You know, when I agreed to run for this seat, I never expected I would be competing against another person. A seat on the city council of a small town is somewhere between the dog catcher and the tax assessor. When Mr. Digby announced he would also be running for the position, I'll have to admit, I had second thoughts about the whole thing."

Struthers leaned back in his chair, crossed his arms and gave me a gentle smile. "I'd be hard pressed to provide so much for your article. I'm a pretty simple guy, you know. I work. I help people. I go to church. I spend time with my family."

"Mr. Digby is a salesman," I said.

"That he is. I suppose I could give you my recipe for Coca-Cola Burgers. It's nothing special, but my kids seem to enjoy it. Of course you have to measure the ingredients just as it says, or it won't come out right."

He pulled out a pad of paper from a desk drawer and started listing ingredients.

"Now, when your readers make this be sure to tell them it's important to baste the burgers." He ripped off the note and handed it to me.

"Thanks, I will." I put the recipe in my notebook along with the legal pad. "Was there anything else you wanted to share?"

"Oh you mean some sort of grilling advice that will cause people to vote for me?"

"Yes." I readied myself to write.

"Uh, stay away from the side of the grill where the smoke is drifting."

I stopped and looked up. Drummond grinned.

He put his hands up in the air and shrugged. "All I've got."

Even though his contribution was much shorter than Baxter Digby's, I already knew who I would vote for.

My phone rang in my purse. "Betsy." The familiar voice of Aunt Maggie rang in my ears. "I need you to come over to my house."

I placed my hand over the phone.

"Sorry," I said to Struthers.

"No problem. I look forward to the article."

I nodded and stepped outside the auto repair shop.

"What's the matter?"

"Uh ... I need you to talk to Danny."

"Why?"

"I don't know. He just says he has to talk to you."

"Okay. Put him on the phone." My cousin Danny was an adult with Down Syndrome, and when he got his heart set on something, he could be pretty stubborn about it.

"I can't," Maggie said.

"Why not?"

"He wants to speak to you in person."

I glanced at my watch, and placed my hand on the small of my aching back. I stretched as the baby shifted.

"Seriously?"

"Yes. I wouldn't be calling, but he insists on seeing you in person."

I sighed. I had planned to sneak a nap in under the ceiling fan with the air conditioner on "arctic blast".

"Betsy?"

"Yes. I'm getting in my car right now. I should be there in five minutes."

"Five minutes" she repeated after me. As she hung up, I heard laughter in the background. Probably from one of the annoying sitcoms Danny liked to watch. He was the only person I knew with the complete Steve Urkel collection on DVD.

As I started the car, the radio blared to life.

"...And the clouds in the Gulf continue to form. With a more defined structure, we expect to send a C-130 Hercules airplane in to look at the eye. Listeners need to be prepared and possibly evacuate. Please stay tuned for important weather information."

I would have to check NUTV at Maggie's house to see if Hurricane Hal was giving a report. I was so happy to see Hal on the local weather broadcast. Last Thanksgiving Leo graciously filled in for him when he had the flu. It was not an experience that turned out well for any of us. Of course, it was also when I found out we were expecting a baby. I guess it wasn't all bad.

Now Leo was working at the weather bureau full-time and with a potential hurricane in the Gulf he was once again putting in long hours.

As we sat, month by month, watching our baby grow, we discussed the reality that our bundle of joy would be due in hurricane season. Some years the months from June to the end of October were quiet in Texas, and other years we experienced storms like Katrina. I just hoped and prayed that this was an uneventful year. With the boys at camp, I wasn't comfortable having our family so far apart. If there was going to be a crisis, would they have a set of procedures they followed up at camp? Was there some sort of storm shelter Tyler and Zach could go to?

I thought of the terrible things that could happen to them up there. I was starting to hyperventilate and the baby was becoming restless. Trying to shake it off, I jumped when the phone jangled next to me.

"Betsy? Are you doing okay?" Leo said on the other end.

"Do you know what kind of storm plan they have up at the boy's camp?"

"Um, no, but I'm sure they have one. It's a state regulation that a summer camp has to have an emergency protocol."

"Are you sure?"

"Yes. Betsy, I'm sure. You don't sound good. Are you in labor?"

"No." The baby kicked. "I don't think so anyway. I just started feeling panicky about the boys being so far away and the weather in the Gulf."

"I know."

"Maybe I should drive up there and get them," I volunteered.

"How are you going to do that? You're almost to full term. What would do if you went into labor on the road? Besides, all that sitting in the car isn't good for you anyway."

I sighed, feeling every inch of my body radiating with sweat and exhaustion.

"But what about the boys?"

"Bets. Listen to me. They will be all right."

"What if they get a tornado? That camp is just a step above a trailer park."

"Bets. You're making yourself crazy. Listen, I would go get them if I could, but I just can't get the time to do it right now. It's the Black Friday of meteorology."

"We can't leave them stranded up there either."

Leo was silent. He knew I was right. He knew better than most people what kind of storm was headed toward us.

"I know this is probably a bad time to tell you this, but guess what? I get to go with the 53rd Weather Reconnaissance Squadron in a plane right into the center of the storm. Isn't that exciting?"

If he was waiting for a positive response from me, it just wasn't going to happen.

"You can't."

"But, Betsy..."

"Leo. You just can't. What if something were to happen?"

"Nothing is going to happen."

"I don't know if you noticed this or not, but you could be up in the cloud and I could be down here in labor alone. Tell them you'll go next time."

"It's a short little trip. There's so much I'll be able to see."

"I don't like the idea of it. Please don't go."

"Betsy..."

"I'm at Aunt Maggie's. Danny needs me. We'll talk about this later."

CHAPTER 4

As I pulled into Aunt Maggie's driveway, I noticed an abundance of cars parked on the street. The strange phone call began to make sense to me along with the muffled laughter in the background and Danny's unreasonable request. I was being set up.

I sighed and wrestled to get out of the car feeling the two-inch elastic waistband that had been sticking to my belly was beginning to roll. Once standing, I yanked at my maternity pants wondering how many people in the house caught sight of my awkward gesture. It was really sweet of them, but all I wanted to do was go home and take a nap, especially after my last conversation. How could Leo want to go flying into a weather system right now? I walked up to the front door and opened it without ringing. A privilege of family.

"Danny?"

"Surprise!"

The front room was, as I had suspected, filled with the women of Pecan Bayou.

I tried to look shocked and happy, and hoped I was pulling it off. Aunt Maggie gave me a big hug and then Danny jumped in, folding his arms around both of us a little too tightly. Danny shouted into my ear. "I was a part of the surprise, Betsy. ""You sure were. You got me."

"I did. I did."

"Come on over here, Betsy. A lot of folks want to talk to you today."

I obediently fell in step behind my aunt. Libby Loper and Ruby Green scooted over to give me a spot between them on the couch. I felt assistance at my elbows once more as they helped me to lower down onto the soft cushions. It was as much work as a plane landing on an aircraft carrier.

"Well you finally made it. We were afraid you were heading straight to the hospital," Ruby said. Ruby, always dressed to match an occasion, had on a baby pink top with baby blue capri pants. Her earrings were little pacifiers. Her hair was done up in a lovely shade of buttercup blond. She had alternating pink and blue fingernails. This was an outfit we would need a picture of for the baby book.

My good friend Elaina, and one of the few women at the shower close to my age, sat over in the corner looking a little uncomfortable. She had her knees pushed together with her hands neatly folded in her lap. Dressed in her patrolman's uniform, she raised one hand in a jerky wave.

"I didn't know we were going to need police coverage for a baby shower," I said.

"Yeah." She nodded. "It could get pretty wild between the 'Baby Name Scramble' and the 'Baby Gift Bingo'. Your dad gave me a couple of hours off, so I could attend the festivities."

Though my dad probably thought of it as a special favor, my friend didn't appear to be all that happy with the deal. Elaina would have preferred to be pulling over a drunk driver than going through this. Of all of the women in the room, she might be able to handle a .38, but really hadn't participated in many of the rituals that women go through. Elaina was single, and her relationship with our local DA was on-again- off-again, so this little hen party was not something she felt a part of.

Mayor Obermyer's wife patted Elaina on her knee. "Don't you worry dear. Your turn is coming. "

"This is just so much fun," she said, her smile a little on the vacant side.

"So how is the romance going with you and our district attorney? " Libby Loper pulled on her turquoise necklace that adorned her beige jean jacket and matching skirt. She looked like she might have just stepped out of one of her father's old cowboy movies.

"Oh everything is fine," Elaina said, her lips thinning.

"Might we be planning a wedding shower for you sometime in the future?" Aunt Maggie said, a little gleam in her eyes.

"Leave her alone ladies," I said. "You're like a bunch of vampires at a blood bank. Give her time. "

"Thanks, Betsy. Although, I do have to admit all this baby stuff does look like fun," Elaina repeated, more convincingly this time.

"Which part? The massive weight gain, the backache, or that you don't sleep for the last three months?"

Aunt Maggie came over and patted my hand. "Now, now, Betsy. This will all be over before you know it, and you won't even remember how miserable you are now. I promise."

Birdie, the owner of Birdie's Diner, brought over a gift bag with a yellow giraffe on it. "Go ahead and open mine, Betsy. I can't stay. My new boyfriend needs me down at the diner. We're putting a chicken he made entirely out of soup cans on the roof. He has a knack for crafts, you know." I had been so absorbed in my own life, I wasn't aware of Birdie's new boyfriend.

"Hmmm. Next time I'm in the diner I want to hear all about this new man in your life."

"He's wonderful," she said. "I never thought I'd find love again this late in the game."

"How did you meet him?"

"I'm a little embarrassed about this, but everyone's doing it."

I waited for her to say she met him online.

"I went down to the bingo game at the Our Lady of Guadalupe in Andersonville. I heard it was a great place to meet people. I'm not even Catholic, but they let me play anyway. He sat right next me and the next I knew we were dating."

"So romantic," I said.

"You don't know the half of it." She smiled.

I reached into the gift bag and pulled out a set of yellow booties and t-shirt that emblazoned with *Birdie's Diner—Fine Dining for the Family*.

"Very nice. Thank you," I said. Birdie gave me a quick hug.

"I'm off. Time to get that chicken on the roof."

"You have to open my gift next," Ruby said. She reached over and grabbed an ornately decorated bag and put it in my hands. I was ecstatic that we were going straight to the pink and blue boxes and bags sitting on the fireplace and skipping all the silly baby shower games.

"Now Ruby, we can't start with gifts first. We have to play 'Baby Name Scramble'!" my aunt said, rubbing her hands together in excitement. I longed for my nap.

An hour later, I finally got to opening the gifts. One by one the ladies of Pecan Bayou gave me everything I would ever need. It had been so many years since I had a little one in the house, I was starting all over. Their gifts were wonderful, especially seeing as I hadn't felt like shopping for the baby in the last couple of weeks.

"Danny, where is your gift? Did you put it in the pile with the others?" Maggie asked.

"No. I did not," Danny said between handfuls of Fritos.

"Well go and get it. People are starting to leave."

"No. The baby hasn't come in on angel wings yet. I want to give my gift to the baby."

"Yes, but this is a time when we get Betsy presents to get ready for the baby."

He spoke to my aunt slowly as if he felt she was not comprehending. "That baby isn't here, yet. I will give my gift to the baby when he's here. That way he can say thank you."

"I hope you can wait, Betsy," Maggie said.

I stretched and yawned and then turned toward my cousin. "Makes perfect sense to me."

CHAPTER 5

As I finally made my way home from the shower, I drove by the town square where bronze Charlie Loper now stood proudly with his giant fiberglass horse. A couple of boys were playing near the horse and one ventured on top of it. Great, now they could classify the monstrosity as a playground as well. Someone in a white pickup parked across the street was taking pictures. I just hoped Pecan Bayou wasn't in the running for a world's ugliest town competition.

I continued down the street, driving past the new Super Stay Motel. As I drove by, Baxter Digby stepped out of his silver Escalade which sported a Digby campaign bumper sticker on the back. What would he be doing at the motel in the middle of the day? As if he knew I was watching him, he looked around from side to side. I couldn't exactly duck down in my car, so I jerked my gaze forward. When I pulled up to the stop sign on the corner, I looked back in my rearview mirror. Digby took out a card and placed it in the door slot of one of the motel rooms. Maybe he and his wife were meeting in the middle of the day for a rendezvous? An afternoon in the Super Stay didn't really ring romance in my head. Cheap, maybe, but romance, never. Maybe it wasn't his wife on the other side of that door.

I suddenly wished I hadn't witnessed Digby's possible indiscretion. This was just the kind of news Rocky would love to get his hands on. A city council member having an affair? It was ten times better than the bake sale going on down at the VFW. I didn't feel I needed to add "scooping to the tabloids" to my work resume, so I just kept driving. There was probably a reasonable explanation for this. Maybe it was a candidate planning meeting. I had trouble believing that. Whatever it was, I decided to keep it to myself for now.

A few minutes later, as I carried in my shower gifts, my cell phone began ringing in my purse, which was still in the car. I hurried to my car to reach over the driver's seat and answer it before it went to voice mail.

"Mom! Hey Mom. Have you heard about the storm?" Zach was calling from camp again. I still hadn't called the counselor to ask about the poker game and to send more funds for my high rollers. Then again he might be calling to tell me the camp was sending everybody home.

"Yes. It's all over the news here, too. Your dad and I have discussed a plan for you guys."

"Good. Who's going to pick us up?"

"Actually you're probably out of the storm's path that far upstate and safer than if you would be in Pecan Bayou."

"Is that what Leo saw on the screens at the weather bureau?"

"Yes. I've been watching it too, but I can't drive there and get you because there's a chance I could go into labor on the way."

"Cool."

"You won't think it's very cool if you have to deliver your little brother or sister."

"Mom. I'm a scout. We get all kinds of training."

I would be really surprised if there was an obstetrics badge, I thought. "I'm glad to know that, but I'll just use a doctor instead. We also think it would be a better idea if you were to stay there."

"Mom," he begged, his voice catching in between soprano and alto.

"It will be okay, Zach. Have your counselors talked to you about a storm plan?"

"Yeah. We have a plan. We've been doing weather drills. All that stuff."

"Now you listen to them, because though your dad says the weather isn't coming your way, we still want to make sure you know what to do in an emergency."

"I'm listening."

"Great. Maybe we should be calling each other at least once a day."

"Sure, and if you have a baby, pleeeeease call me."

As if I would forget. "You know I will. Love you. Oh, and no more gambling."

"Love you, too. No more gambling, and I can't wait to see my new brother or sister. When will you tell me what it is?"

"You'll find out soon enough."

CHAPTER 6

By the time I crawled into bed that evening, I was beyond tired. I expected Leo at eleven o'clock, so I took the extra time to relax. Butch lay snoring on the carpet next to the bed. Who knew a dog could be so loud?

I opened my copy of *What to Expect When You're Expecting*. This had been a gift to me when I was expecting Zach and was the ultimate pregnant book informing you month by month what the heck that kid was doing to your body. This late in the book I wondered if they started omitting the scary stuff. There would be nothing about the panicky drive to the hospital and the eventual hours of requesting more painkillers. Nobody would buy the book if they knew the real truth. My eyelids were starting to become heavy, and I set my reading on my belly. Maybe the baby would enjoy it.

"They're all waiting." I heard a voice that came in on the wind. Then, I noticed the corners of the room. They were softer and less in focus.

"Who's waiting?" I asked.

"They are, of course." Standing next to the box that contained the pieces of our changing table I recognized Martha Hoffman, the town librarian. As usual, she looked impatient with me. She was also dead.

"Martha? I mean Ms. Hoffman?"

"Is there something wrong with your eyes?"

"No. It's just that, well, you're dead. How can you be talking to me if you're dead?"

"So many questions. I always hated questions. What's the capital of Brazil? Where do I find Shakespeare's plays? What is electricity? Questions! Questions! Questions! Who freakin' cares? Good grief, can't people look things up?"

I don't recall having had this long of a conversation when Martha was living. I also never would've predicted that if a ghost were going to visit me it would be the angry librarian. She wore her functional cardigan sweater over wool tweed skirt, accompanied by her sensible shoes with thick heels. She adjusted her red framed glasses on her nose.

"Bootsy Lindeman, did you get my message?"

As she had in life, she screwed up my name. In her final days she created all kinds of names for me, none of them correct. She knew my name all along, and we both knew it. By making me so unimportant that remembering my name was a chore, she kept me in my place, like a book on the shelf.

"Oh. Yes. They're all waiting. The thing is you never told me who was waiting."

"You're a policeman's daughter. I think you can figure this out. For some reason these idiots think it's important that they talk to you."

"Who? Who needs to talk to me? Is this some crazy pregnant dream?"

"No. But it's important for you to listen, Bootsy. Listen and follow what they say, and don't let the dreams swirl around in that empty head too much. You're dizzy enough. When it's time to take action, you need to blow on out of there. Step out of the frame."

"Huh?" She was beginning to sound like Leo talking in weather patterns. Maybe this woman was my subconscious so inundated with meteorology talk that now these terms were creeping into my nightmares. Characters in my dreams were even talking about the weather.

I never told Leo that I rarely watched The Weather Channel until I started dating him. He would be heartbroken to know that. In my mind, either it rains or it doesn't. It never really concerned me before. I had The Weather Channel bookmarked on my cable now, that was for sure.

"Goodbye Bootsy. Don't screw this up." Martha Hoffman started dissolving in the corner. She was there, and then she was gone.

"Betsy?" I felt Leo getting into bed next to me. "Are you okay Bets?" His hands slipped around me.

"Sure. I was asleep." I said, looking at him through half-open eyes.

"You were having a full-fledged conversation. Did you know you were talking in your sleep?"

"Yeah? What was I saying?"

"Something about the Weather Channel."

"It's so silly what comes out of your mouth when you're dreaming," I said.

CHAPTER 7

The next morning I sipped my coffee, feeling groggy—the effects of working my way through an entire quart of Ben & Jerry's Chunky Monkey after Leo came to bed. I couldn't get dead Martha Hoffman out of my head, and the best activity I could think of to eradicate her creepy visit was to consume massive amounts of ice cream.

Leo was up and in the shower, getting ready to take off for another day of storm tracking. I had my laptop on the kitchen table and was putting finishing touches on the barbecue recipes for the city council grill-off. A knock at the door made me jump. A face, eerily distorted by the beveled glass, peered through at me.

"Betsy?" Whatever it was, it knew my name. Was Martha using the front door now?

"Mind if I come in darlin'?"

"Hey Dad," I said, relief in my voice. "Come on in. Have you had your coffee?"

"I could use another cup," he said, pulling up a chair. He took off his hat and placed it on the table. "You should know I spent part of the night last night worrying about you. What with Leo gone so much working the storm, I started to have thoughts you would go into labor and for some reason not be able to call anybody."

It was good to know that even a seasoned parent like my father had middle of the night panic attacks. It helped me not to feel so guilty about my own anxiety over the boys being so far away.

"Last I heard women going to labor do not lose their abilities to call someone. I know the entire police force has me on their radar, thanks to you."

"Well, sure."

"If I can't get Leo, you and Aunt Maggie are on speed dial." As if they weren't already.

"That gives this sleepy old man some peace of mind."

Leo tromped down the stairs from the bedroom and poured himself a cup of coffee, the smell of fresh aftershave drifting through the room.

"Good morning, Judd."

"Morning Leo. And, how is the storm chaser today?"

"Busy."

"Somehow, I figured that."

"Yes sir. It looks like we might have a big one on our hands," he said searching in the cupboard for a cereal bar. I finished those off two days ago.

I couldn't help noticing how excited my husband was about a destructive storm on its way. It could impact the people in Texas both financially and mentally. It was a little twisted, but I understood.

"Yeah, yeah, Lester Jibbets was just saying the woods of Pecan Bayou are getting quiet. The animals know when a storm is comin'. "

"He said that? If we could just get Lester on the payroll at the weather bureau," Leo said, still searching.

"He's too busy with his port-a-potty empire to work for you. I just hope that with all this running around you're doing for the storm that you don't forget my baby here is about to have a baby."

"It's crossed my mind a time or two."

"Well that's good to hear."

"You have to admit I am juggling quite a bit right now. This storm could be another Katrina." Leo walked over to the refrigerator and looked inside, pushing aside plastic containers and ketchup bottles. "You know, maybe I'll just pick up a biscuit on the way," he said, closing the door.

My father continued. "Don't make me do SWAT team drills to get her to the hospital."

"Your so-called SWAT team practice mostly involves running in and out of Earl's Coffee," I said. "Their timing was great right up until Earl took out that fresh batch of coffee cake."

"You know we still need to talk." I said, reminding Leo of our phone conversation before the baby shower.

"And we will, but I have to get going right now," he said, kissing me on the cheek and heading out the front door.

My father's walkie talkie cackled on his shoulder.

"Judd? Are you there?" He tapped on his radio.

"Yes Mrs. Thatcher. I'm here having coffee at Betsy's."

"Oh. How is she doing? Is the baby coming?"

"She's fine. Just checking on her. "

"Wonderful. You tell her to put her feet up. She needs to take it easy because we don't want to hurry that little guy."

"I'll be sure to share that with her. Is there something you need, Mrs. Thatcher?"

"Oh. I almost forgot." Mrs. Thatcher chuckled on the other side of the line. "We have a bit of a situation, Judd."

"And what would that be?"

"I need you to get over to the town square to the Charlie Loper statue."

"This is a first. Don't tell me the statue is disturbing the peace."

"You could say that."

"What's going on?"

"Well, for the first time in more than one hundred years we have a horse thief among us."

"Pardon?"

"Charlie's horse. It's been stolen."

Wanting to be a part of tracking down the first horse thief in a century, I grabbed my flip flops and followed dad to the crime scene in the town square. Even with the heat, there was a crowd gathered around the statue. I spotted Rocky, the ever-vigilant reporter making his way to the front. Rocky might be an old guy, but a good news story wasn't going to slow him down. Behind him, Stan from NUTV followed with a camera on his shoulder. This was big news when both outlets of the Pecan Bayou media showed up at once.

"Unbelievable. You'd think these people would all have jobs to go to," Dad said, a little too loudly.

As we came closer to the statue of Charlie, we found him standing his corner, but now instead the horse reigns in his outstretched three fingers, the pointer and ring finger had broken off when the thief disconnected the reigns. Charlie Loper was effectively flipping off anyone who passed by him.

"There goes the tourism dollar," I said.

"Who in their right mind would want to steal a giant fiberglass horse? What is this world coming to?" Judd said.

"Do you think they can glue some fingers back on it?" I asked.

"Hell if I know."

"Why don't I call Libby to see if they have any leather riding gloves in the museum that we could put on him," I said.

"Yeah, and while you're at it, tell her that her daddy's horse has been stolen. She's going to love hearing that."

My father walked over to where the horse had been standing. He drew in a breath and then expelled it as he looked around. "I can see some tire tracks where the perpetrator pulled up on the curb."

I was dialing Libby on my phone, but turned around to see her approaching us, her phone ringing. I ended the call as Ruby Green stepped out of the crowd to walk with her. Obviously I hadn't been the only one to think of calling Libby. The Charlie Loper Museum and Ranch was a few miles outside Pecan Bayou so she made good time getting here. Libby looked as if she jumped in her Caddy with her robe still on reminding me of the first time I met her. On that day she had been under the influence of some sort of drug and was hanging out of her upstairs window shouting at me to clean her house.

Libby placed her hand on the statue as if he were a living being.

"Oh, Daddy. I'm so sorry about this. I know how much you loved Ol' Bess."

We stood awkwardly by while she conversed with the dark brown lump of metal. As she started to give it a kiss, I spoke up.

"I was just wondering. How heavy was the horse?"

"Yes," my father added. "How many guys would it take to load it onto a truck?"

Libby turned away from her father's bronzed face. "I don't know. It could be pretty tough to lift. That's why we put wheels under the hooves. We needed to move it around to dust it at the museum."

"So somebody might have rolled him right up a ramp into a truck."

"That means it could be a person acting solely on their own," Rocky said, now standing behind us. "Which brings us back to the first question. What kind of lunatic steals a giant toy horse?"

"Quite possibly one of our fine citizens of Pecan Bayou," my father said, gesturing to the crowd of onlookers.

"I was really going for the drifter angle," Rocky said.

"Well, if it was someone here in town, it would pretty hard to hide a life-sized horse," I said.

"Unless of course our thief stole Ol' Bess and plans to put it in a Putt-Putt golf course or some drugstore cowboy tourist trap."

"There is another dude ranch in the valley who's been stealin' my business," Libby said. "Maybe they stole Daddy's horse as well."

"Will you be using the same guidelines for punishment they did one hundred years ago?" Rocky asked.

"No," my father said flatly. "We will not be stringing anybody up for this."

Rocky scowled, disappointed he didn't have a hanging to cover.

I looked over and realized Stan had been filming the entire conversation for NUTV. I nudged my father, who then walked over and put his hand on the camera lens.

"Not right now Stan. Can't you see Miss Libby is in her robe?"

"Will there be a press conference?"

"Not likely," he said. "And don't be using that film without my permission, ya hear?"

Stan shut off the camera. "Back to the farm report, I guess." It was his top rated show.

CHAPTER 8

Once Libby brought out some leather riding gloves and put them over Charlie's poor mutilated hand, the crowd thinned out. I started to head for home, but couldn't stop thinking of Benny's Cocoa Pecan Pie. I stopped over at Benny's Barbecue, though he hadn't officially started serving lunch yet. Benny was in the back, turning pieces of chicken. From the sweat on his brow, it looked like it was over a hundred degrees by the stove. Benny took a towel and swiped at his face.

"Hey Betsy," he called through the rectangular opening between the kitchen and front counter. I noticed an attractive brunette waitress standing in the corner, texting on her phone. She was a new addition to the staff, which was unusual in a family-run business.

"Hi, Benny. You've hired help."

"Oh." He came out, wiping his hands on the towel. "Sorry." He gestured the waitress over, and she jammed her phone in her apron pocket. Benny put his arm around the woman whose uniform looked a little tight around the bust line. Who was I to judge? None of my clothes had fit for months. Right now, I was walking around in the equivalent of a flowered tent that hung over shorts.

"This is Sasha. She's my new waitress. I just hired her."

"Nice to meet you Sasha." I nodded and then looked to Benny. "I didn't know you hired outside of family."

"Well, Celia and I have handled it for years, but Sasha here came in and asked for a job. Celia's studying for her accounting exam, so it just worked out."

"Good for her," I said.

"Sure. Celia kept the books here since we bought this place. She has a talent for it."

Sasha smiled and turned to me. "I'm newly divorced." As if needing a rim shot, she snapped her gum.

"I'm sorry to hear that."

"Don't be."

"Okay." An awkward pause settled between us so I tried to get my mission back on track. "So, I'm here to..."

"Nope. I already know. I have my psychic hat on today." From under the counter Benny pulled out a brown paper bag, folded down neatly at the top, with my name on it. "Benny's Cocoa Pecan Pie. On the house."

I gasped. Was I that predictable?

"You've been in here practically every day since you found out you were pregnant. Benny's pie is your craving. Do you know what it is? The cocoa. It's a triple cocoa blend I order special from King Arthur Flour. You can't just get it anywhere. No ma'am. I'm so proud that I've been such a big part in making this baby."

That didn't sound right, somehow, but I liked Benny too much to say anything.

"How much longer?" Sasha asked.

"Oh..." I ran my hand along the curve that was my baby. "...not too much longer. Probably a couple of weeks."

"Is this your first?"

"No. I have a son and a stepson."

"The new America. Blended families," Benny said, as if explaining current sociological trends was also something she needed to know to be a waitress.

Sasha, who had been leaning on the counter, bosom spilling over, now stood up straight. "Yeah, well at least my ex and I didn't have any kids, although there were times I thought it might be nice."

"Children are wonderful," I said.

"Maybe so, but my ex-husband was a real head case. Always kept talking about how much he wanted to go live out in the country somewhere. Wanted to homestead or something. Like, who does that in this century? I told him, if I'm not within five miles of a mani-pedi it just ain't worth it. You know, you never know who you're married to until you're married to him."

"Ain't that the truth," Benny said.

"I thought I was marrying some up-and-coming artist. Then I saw his work. All I had to do was see how he signed every painting to know that the guy wasn't firing on all cylinders."

"How did he sign his work?" I asked.

"He signed it with his initials and a smiley face. A smiley face? Seriously? What professional artist signs his work with a smiley face? A third grader? I finally told him to pack up and go live out in the country somewhere. Paint by candlelight in a log cabin. That's what he wanted. Where did we live? A lousy rental house on the other side of town. When he wouldn't leave, I packed up and left. I'm in a better place now." She kissed Benny on the cheek and went into the kitchen.

Benny and I exchanged glances. "Well, at least now you can give Hooters a run for its money. Thanks for the free pie!" I said, grabbing my bag and heading out the door.

As I unlocked the door at home, I decided to go upstairs and sit in the newly decorated nursery to eat my pie in private. Yes, not all of the furniture was assembled and in place yet, but it still felt like a special room. This would be the baby's room and sitting in it made me happy, peaceful even. Once I got myself situated in the rocker, Butch came over and put his large head on my knee. His big brown eyes gazed adoringly up to me—or the pie. I couldn't be sure.

"Not for you, boy. Sorry." All for Mama, I thought. I took one bite of Benny's pie and sighed. He was right. It was the cocoa. My sigh turned into a yawn. The house was quiet and still. As I glanced up at the decals of teddy bears on the wall, I wondered what this child would be like.

This pregnancy was so different from my last. My first husband, Barry, was haunted by the idea of Down Syndrome. He had never been comfortable with having Danny in the family. I would catch him staring at Danny when he didn't think anyone was watching him. As we came closer to the due date, Barry became distant, working long hours and rarely returning a phone call during the day. By the time I was ready to have our baby, Barry was long gone, disappearing into the night on the premise of making an unnecessary trip to the drugstore. I didn't see him again until years later.

Leo was a distinct contrast to Barry. Where Barry could be very secretive, Leo was open. Barry feared the unknown; Leo welcomed it.

I thought about Sasha Holman and her comments about her ex-husband. It was true; you don't always know who you are marrying until you've lived with them for a while. She didn't know her husband wanted to live a more simple life in the country. I felt sure I knew Leo, but still in the back of my mind I questioned if he missed living in Dallas. He was a part of the weather bureau in this area and he was closer to the action of hurricane season, but did he miss his job up there?

In our marriage, so far he had made all of the significant compromises. When we met he had a job in Dallas, and I had a life in Pecan Bayou. I could have written my column anywhere, for any newspaper willing to carry *The Happy Hinter*. Still though, he found a job in meteorology in this part of Texas with the weather bureau. That was Leo, willing to give up something dear to him to make our lives work together.

After finishing the mouth-watering pie, I returned the container to the bag. I stood up and turned the white plastic knob on the baby's mobile. The gentle tinkle of the music box filled the air. I watched the little stars appliqued on the blue denim squares go around and around. The mobile could have been pink or blue, but I didn't want to reveal the sex of our baby. It was our little secret. As I listened to the lilting notes of the lullaby, I sat back in the rocking chair and hummed along.

I found myself getting sleepy as I rocked back and forth. I drifted off to sleep.

"Betsy?" I heard a gentle voice in my ear. I lifted my head and Oliver Canfield came into focus. He was my husband's old business partner and the first body I ever stumbled upon.

Aunt Maggie and I had been in the old tuberculosis hospital hunting for ghosts when I found Oliver Canfield's shoe. I screamed when I realized his foot, a ghastly gray-green, was still inside it.

Today, he wore the same suit he had on the day I found him dead, but today it looked clean and ironed. Obviously there must be a vibrant dry cleaning business on the other side. He turned his head slightly to the side and then grinned, a twinkle in his eye. Oliver had been a con man extraordinaire, and I was sure this must have been the smile he used to bilk women out of their life savings.

"Oliver?"

"You remember me. That's so kind of you."

"Aren't you dead?"

"Technically, yes. But, you see I'm right here now."

He was right. He was standing in front as solid as any living person. I still wasn't sure if I trusted myself with his powers of persuasion. He squatted down, putting his hands over each arm of the rocking chair. I felt surrounded and began to panic.

"You did me a favor bringing my killer to justice. I wanted to thank you for that. We both know I didn't really deserve it. I wasn't such a good guy in life. Never thought my wrong would be made right by a woman."

"Uh. You're welcome."

"Your baby will be here soon."

"Yes."

"Barry never had the heart of a father. I'm glad you've changed course and have a new life."

"Yeah. Thanks."

"A better life. I heard once our existence is but a crack between two eternities. Who said that?"

"Uh. I don't think I know." The phone ringing down the hall jolted me out of my sleep. Oliver's hands were no longer on the arms of the chair. When I looked down, Butch's head was resting on my lap. I pulled myself up out of the rocker and headed for the telephone. Butch trotted along behind me. I grabbed the phone.

"Hey is Leo there by chance?"

"No," I said stifling a yawn. "He's not. Can I take a message?"

"This is J.J. over at the weather service. We have the okay from the Air Force 53rd Weather Reconnaissance Squadron for him to go on the ride into the cloud. I know he'll be happy. It's quite an opportunity." I froze as I listened to J.J.'s excitement.

"I see. I hope he has a very good parachute."

"The only thing that gets a parachute is the dropsonde, the little device that will measure the wind speed. If they get into trouble they are better off ditching the plane."

"I'll be sure and let him know. He's been difficult to stay in touch with because the battery on his cell phone keeps running down. I'll tell him you called."

"Great. Thanks Betsy." After hearing this, I wondered if a new pint of Ben and Jerry's was warranted.

I heard the creak of the door opening downstairs. "Bets? Are you up there?"

What was Leo doing home this time of day? Had something happened with the boys? Maybe there was something going around with the men of Pecan Bayou, and he wanted to rent a room at the Super Stay Motel? Between the sleepiness and the pie crumbs all over me, boy was he going to be disappointed.

"Yes, I'm up here."

"Well, come on down," he said, in his best Don Pardo voice. "Do I have a surprise for you."

I made my way downstairs to find Leo in the living room surrounded by a number of pastel gift bags and boxes.

"What's this?"

"They had a baby shower for me."

"Who did?"

"The weather bureau. They have a policy that it doesn't matter if you are a man or a woman, if you are expecting a first baby they give you a shower."

Their generosity was wonderful, but after Aunt Maggie's shower for me, all I could think about was another set of thank you notes to write.

"Wow. I can't believe they gave a baby shower." I wondered if they made him play the stupid games. I could just see the egghead meteorologists playing pin the diaper on the baby doll. Don't get me wrong, I was grateful, just tired.

"Between the two showers, there's nothing we need to buy for the baby."

"You're right. I think we're good to go."

Leo came up behind me and placed his hands on my rounded stomach. As his touch lingered on my skin, I felt the baby kick.

"Wow," he whispered into my ear. "We either have a football player or a Rockette in there."

"The baby has been very active today, probably due to my daily piece of Benny's Cocoa Pecan Pie."

"I'm going to have to buy a percentage of Benny's Barbecue with all the trips you're making down there."

"Money well spent. So..." I hated to tell him. "J.J. called."

"Really? So soon?" His excited tone reminded of a kid at Christmas.

"Yes. You're approved to fly into the storm."

He rocked both fists in the air. "Yes!"

"Leo," I tried to sound patient. "You know how I feel about this."

Leo turned me around and took my hands and squeezed gently.

"I know, but an opportunity like this doesn't come along every day. These guys are flying right into a hurricane. How can I pass that up?"

My patience was about to leave the building. "I'll tell you how. I don't know if you've noticed this, but we are about to have a baby. I need you here and not up in the clouds hanging out with some crazy pilot with a death wish."

"And I will be here, sweetie. Believe me, I am so ready for this."

"So you're putting your life in danger? Is this how you're ready for this?"

"Bets ... It's just one day. I'll be back before you know it. The baby is a couple of weeks off yet. What are the chances? Eat your pie, take naps, and visit Aunt Maggie."

If it were only that easy. I really wanted him to pursue his dream, but I just couldn't deal with the idea of him being in so much danger right before our baby was to be born. I'd done the single mom thing, and I wasn't ready to jump back into it. I didn't think what I was asking was too much of him. It was a perfectly realistic request, and in my present state it was more than reasonable.

He held my hands close to his chest. His blue eyes peered into mine, weakening my determination. "Betsy, if this upsets you this much I can tell them no. But things like this are going to happen in our lives. Sometimes, you just have to trust me. I'm not planning on leaving you. There is no place I would rather be than right here at your side, and I'll fight through a thousand storms to get back here. I just really need you to be okay with this."

I was sure of it now. My husband was out of his head. Still though, I understood what he was trying to tell me. It was the same kind of drive that I had when I was told to stay away from a crime scene. Sometimes, you just can't help yourself. As if insanity was contagious, I muttered one word.

"Okay."

"What?"

"I'm giving in."

Leo pulled me closer and kissed me tenderly, helping me to forget for just a moment the unbridled fear I felt with him flying into a hurricane. When he gently released me, he spoke softly. "This is why I love you, Betsy Livingston Fitzpatrick."

I could only hope we made the right decision.

CHAPTER 9

The next morning, I slept in after staying up late to finish Rocky's grilling-with-the-candidates article. I awoke alone since Leo had left during the night to reach Biloxi, Mississippi by eight o'clock the next morning. It felt so much like the day Barry left.

To keep my mind off of Leo flying into a hurricane, I started to assemble the changing table I had ordered online. It appeared to be a pretty simple do-it-yourself job—one that any respectable Happy Hinter should be able to handle.

Once I tore the box open, I determined the task wasn't as simple as I expected, since the foreign manufacturer who sent it to me hadn't included enough bolts. As I pieced together furniture components, I bounced between worrying about the baby, fretting about Leo, and wondering whether the boys had given up poker and were paying attention during weather drills. Putting this piece of necessary baby furniture together was the only thing that was keeping me from breaking down with a Hallmark movie and half the refrigerator.

A search through both the garage and the junk drawer yielded nothing that would work for the changing table, so I decided to drive over to Pecan Bayou Hardware for replacement parts. I went back to the nursery to grab the directions to use for reference.

As looked at the pieces spread out on the floor, I became more determined to get this job done. The table was a lovely shade of dark cherry wood with three drawers on the left side and a convenient hamper on the right. Once this was put together, the nursery would almost be complete. There were only seven pieces to assemble, and I was ready to immerse myself in the project.

The road was already glistening from the heat as I drove the five blocks to the hardware store. My eyes riveted from the gleam of the street to red and blue flashing lights. A Pecan Bayou cruiser was parked in front of the Cattleman's Call Steakhouse.

Deciding the changing table could wait, I pulled up behind the police car. Elaina was taking notes as she listened to the restaurant owner, Lonnie Carello. As I exited my car, I noticed there was something different about the eating establishment. I couldn't remember seeing two large poles planted in front of it. Had there been a sign there? That didn't make sense because there was already a wooden sign with a longhorn painted on it up near the road.

"So when do you think it was stolen?" Elaina asked.

"Had to have been during the night. We've been doing renovations and the workers took off some time after five." Mr. Carello ran his hand through his thick black hair. He was in his mid-forties and slightly heavy for a man his size. He wore a double knit polo shirt that had puddles of perspiration soaking through it.

I looked at the poles again.

"Who the hell steals a plastic cow? That's what I want to know. Who would want the thing? Seriously? There's something wrong with this two-bit town. When I agreed to help out my partner I had no idea how weird you people were are. This never would have happened in Chicago."

Elaina's lips thinned as she peered up at where the cow formerly grazed mid-air. "It is a strange item to steal."

"We have computers, flat screen TVs and all sorts of things that normal criminals steal. I seriously doubt there's a black market for plastic cows."

"Maybe somebody else with a restaurant that sells steaks wants one," I said from behind them.

"Oh great, don't tell me this is another member of your so-called law enforcement team."

"Only when we let her," Elaina said. "Mr. Carello, this is Betsy Livingston, the Happy Hinter."

"Hope you got the hint on what made you in the family way."

What a jerk. I scowled and squinted at him. "Yep. Got that one down."

"So what are you going to do?" Mr. Carello asked, turning back to Elaina. "Check Ebay to see if my cow shows up? That is, if your police department even has internet."

Lonnie Carello shook his head in disgust. He had taken over Cattleman's Call a few months ago after his business partner, Ron Neuwitt, retired.

The first thing Carello did was put up new siding on the old building that used to resemble a log cabin. After that, he gutted most of the inside and put up all new walls. We all hoped he would reopen soon, a restaurant that served T-Bone steaks in Texas was indeed a necessity. The renovations made the restaurant look more like some sort of city sports bar instead of the quaint homey place Ron Neuwitt and his wife had owned and operated for more than thirty years.

Cattleman's Call had been the place to go for special occasions. I remembered my dad bringing me there for my graduation from high school. But Ron Neuwitt was getting old and it was time for him to retire. Lonnie Carello didn't appear much younger than Neuwitt, but clearly had a lot of energy. His personality was the exact opposite of his predecessor, the kind restaurateur. Where Mr. Neuwitt had been kind and savored all things Pecan Bayou, Mr. Carello just wanted to change them.

"You know, I thought I was working well with this community. I never thought one of these yocals would steal my plastic cow. I even tried to employ local craftsmen and planned to have a mural of the town painted on the back wall. I hire this guy who comes in and paints this nice meadow with longhorns in it, and I have to say the painting itself wasn't bad. Then, I look in the corner and right when I'm thinking he's a pretty decent artist, he adds a smiley face. A smiley face in a pasture! It ruined the entire picture. The cows are supposed to be the focal point, not a stupid smiley face. Who does he think he is? Vincent Van Emoticon?"

Before Carello arrived, Cattleman's Call had a bar in the back called the Sheep Dip Lounge, accessed by a separate entrance. Each year, Mr. Neuwitt sponsored a local men's baseball team, aptly named the Dipsticks, which would gather at the Sheep Dip Lounge after every game to celebrate, whether they won or lost. With all of the construction going on, Carello had closed the lounge and dropped and the Dipsticks, so Bubba's Beer and Bait had inherited all the Sheep Dip regulars.

"Do you have any surveillance cameras on the parking lot?" I asked.

"Are you kidding me? In this place? Why would I?" He turned away from me and back to Elaina. "Just find my cow."

"We'll do our best." Elaina snapped her notebook closed. Lonnie Carello threw his hands up and stomped back into his restaurant.

"There goes one unhappy man," I said.

"Pissed off, more like."

"You said it, not me."

"Two ugly fake animals stolen in two days. What are the odds?" Elaina asked.

"You know, I can't be totally sure, but it sounds like to me we have a serial thief with bad taste on our hands."

"Yeah. Maybe it's really the chamber of commerce trying to beautify the place, low-key like."

I shrugged. "I kind of liked the cow. I always thought those tacky pink plastic udders screamed Pecan Bayou."

"Well, someone else liked it too."

Pecan Bayou Hardware was one of the oldest stores in town. The foot-worn floors were constructed from the original oaks that had been in the area over a hundred years ago, and the displays were all handmade. It was in stark contrast to the Superwally with wall-to-wall metal shelving and disturbing fluorescent lights that gave you a headache within fifteen minutes. This place had a history, and with a distinctive smell that made a person think of generations shopping here buying hammers and handsaws. As I picked up the bolts I needed, I had a thought.

"Hey, Bob. What kind of tools would someone need to take down the cow in front of Cattleman's Call?"

Bob put his hand to his chin, extending his lower lip as he thought about my question.

"Hmmm. With enough effort you could probably do it with a hacksaw."

I nodded and felt the baby kick. I was getting pretty close to pie time.

"Has anyone been in here buying a hacksaw in the last week?"

"Nobody lately, but I think everybody around here already has a hacksaw."

"Can you think of anyone who might want to steal the cow from Cattleman's Call?"

"If I had to put money on it, I would say somebody with a restaurant somewhere, or even a guy who wants to mount it over the entrance gate of a big ranch. Maybe Libby Loper stole it to get back at whoever stole her horse. Who knows why people do the things they do. I'm still questioning myself on buying that Smart Car."

Bob had the only Smart Car in town, which was exciting at first. He bragged on how much he saved on gas driving the tiny vehicle, and how it was a wave of the future. That was fine until the high school kids started turning it over as a prank. It was better than cow tipping, one of them had told my father after a night of high school hi-jinx. Now Bob had alarms on the car that went off if you walked within a foot of it and it spent most of its time charging in his garage.

I put my items on the counter. "Is that all for you today?"

"Yes. I'm putting together a changing table for the baby, and it came without bolts."

"Typical." Bob put his finger to his lip and smiled. "Hold on, just one minute." He turned and went into the back room. He returned as promised with a plush toy elephant. It was a promotional item for Blue Elephant Fixative. "For the baby," he said.

"Oh! That reminds me. I need some glue. I accidentally broke a piggy bank that Leo's mother gave us for the baby."

"Well then, I guess it's kismet."

Bob walked over to the shelf that held the Blue Elephant Fixative and grabbed a tube. "Now you be careful with this stuff, young lady. Don't go gluing your fingers together. The only reason you need to be visiting the hospital is to have that young 'un."

"Thanks. I'll do my best."

"Sure, and if you write a handy hint using that stuff, be sure to mention you picked up your tube at Pecan Bayou Hardware."

I'm sure he was thinking of the droves of people that would rush to Pecan Bayou Hardware based on a mention in the Happy Hinter column. Didn't Bob realize he was already the number one destination of every do-it-yourselfer in this town and the next?

"I'll be sure to do that." I heard my phone ring.

I juggled my purse as I extracted the annoying little piece of technology.

"How are you doing Bets?" It was Leo. "We're about to go up, and I just wanted to talk to you one more time." I wish he didn't sound like we'd never see each other again.

"Doing fine. No baby yet." Bob smiled and shook his head.

"Great. Don't overdo it now. You need to save your energy."

"I could say the same of you," I reminded him.

"Yes, you could, but at least I'm not carrying our child."

"Not yet, anyway. Promise me you'll be careful up there. I'm just about to head over..."

Leo finished my sentence. "And get a piece of pie?"

"Why, yes. You must be psychic, Mr. Fitzpatrick."

"I'm a meteorologist. I'm good at predicting patterns."

CHAPTER 10

A half hour later I was driving home and juggling a fresh baked buttery biscuit Benny had thrown in with my pie. Everything was getting greasy and I reached in the bag for a napkin. While waiting at a stoplight, as I wiped butter off the steering wheel, I looked across the intersection at the Super Stay Motel. Baxter Digby's car sat in the parking lot once again. Right next to it was a smaller car, a blue Subaru. It was pretty beat up and looked like someone had tried to scrape off something yellow that had been on the back bumper. Could it belong to the person he was meeting? If Digby were having an affair, it could crush his chances in the city council race. I wondered what that sweet looking woman in the picture in his office would think of her husband's lunch dates? The smaller car didn't look familiar to me, but it was a pretty common make and model.

Once home, I put my bag of bolts and the glue on the kitchen counter. I pulled out the broken pig and after mixing the epoxy, started reassembling the pieces. It came together much better than before, although I could still see a slight crack where the pieces had been joined. I set it on the counter to dry overnight. Pouring myself a glass of milk, I pulled the pie out, grabbed a fork and made my way up to the nursery, Butch bounding on my heels.

After taking only a couple of bites of the pie, I found the biscuit had filled me up. I settled into the rocker and put my feet up on the ottoman. I would put together the changing table in a little bit. Maybe I could do it later this afternoon when I wasn't feeling so tired. I rocked slowly, feeling my whole body sinking down into the soft tan cushions.

"Betsy?"

Vanessa Markham stood in front of me, arms crossed. The fingers of her left hand, adorned with shiny gold fingernails, tapped impatiently on her right arm.

"Really? Sleeping during the day? How very decadent." Vanessa's eyes scanned my rounded shape. "Oh my. You'll never get into a size four now." Not that I had ever been in a size four, except in seventh grade before puberty hit.

Vanessa had been a chick-lit writer who wrote under the pen name Vanessa Scarlet. She and I had never been friends and made the tongues of Pecan Bayou wag once when we had a shouting match in the mall. I remember the day I found her body in the children's section of our local public library. She now stood as Martha Hoffman had, also scowling at me. Even in the afterlife, she didn't like me.

Vanessa wore a white closely fitted pant suit that was probably a size 0, along with a pair of white stiletto heels. Her blond hair was pulled back into a chignon with a few strands flowing around her face. She looked beautiful, and I envied her tiny waist. One good thing about Heaven—no calories. As mean as she was to me, I was a little surprised she was in white at all.

"Why are you here?"

"So, yeah. You figured out who my killer was. I guess I should thank you for that." She gave me a perfunctory smile, as if she'd just put money in the poor box at church.

"Okay."

"You never know about things that are hidden. Everyone has little cracks in them somewhere...just waiting to be discovered."

"Sure."

"That baby already has more style than you ever will."

"Even from the other side, you continue to criticize."

"Some things you don't lose. Of course that extra twenty you've put on is another story..."

Vanessa started to fade as I felt my back starting to ache. I straightened up in the chair, putting my feet on the floor. That was the third strange dream I had experienced in this chair. Maybe I needed a different chair in this room.

I was beginning to feel like Ebenezer Scrooge, but with really rude ghosts. It was nice of Vanessa to thank me even if she probably didn't mean it. I thought about the feeling of her presence. It wasn't like watching a movie—I could see and feel the shape of her. She was so real and so annoying, I shook my head to be rid of her.

I had heard about pregnant women dreaming, but never really experienced anything until now. Why would I be dreaming about murder victims? Wasn't I supposed to be dreaming of walking with the baby in a field of flowers or something? Shouldn't everything be all in soft pastels with Mozart playing gently in the background? My dream visitors felt more like a midnight break-in than a fantasy. I pulled myself up from the chair and glanced at the time. I had been sleeping for over two hours. Shouldn't Leo have called by now? Had he flown into the hurricane yet? It was late in the afternoon, and hopefully he was on the ground and heading back for Pecan Bayou.

Trying not to panic, I called him for a change.

When he answered on the second ring, I was felt a flood of relief that the whole hurricane hunter thing was over, and he was back in contact. "How are you doing, Leo?"

"Are you in labor? I can be there in twenty minutes."

"Leo..."

"I put your to-go bag by the door."

"Leo..."

"Is your cell phone charged?"

"Leo. I'm not having the baby. I just called to check in."

"Oh, sorry. I got busy and forgot to call."

"I noticed. You usually wake me up from my nap and I ended up sleeping a couple of hours."

"That's great, Bets. Just what you should be doing right now. I'm headed home. Hitting some scattered showers, but it shouldn't slow me down too much."

"I'm so glad to hear that. Did you hear the cow was stolen from in front of the Cattleman's Call today?"

His voice took on an added Texas drawl. "What's that you say little lady? Cattle rustlers attacked the one cow herd in front of the steakhouse?" I laughed, resisting the urge to pee. Another bonus of pregnancy.

"Oh, we think it's funny, but the new owner Lonnie Carello is furious. He's sure that losing that plastic cow is the end of his business."

"Well, you never know what triggers a craving for a juicy ribeye. As a matter fact, I could use a big fat steak right now."

"When was the last time you ate something?" I had been so obsessed with my own stomach I didn't think about Leo and his long hours at work. Leo could work all day and forget to eat. That was probably why there wasn't an ounce of fat on him. Thanks to Vanessa for reminding me that I had gained a little more than baby weight.

"Don't worry. I had a sandwich before I left Mississippi. Nate, one of the pilots, wanted to talk to me, so we had lunch together."

"That's good. I had another one of those dreams."

"What dreams?"

"You know, one of *those* dreams." There was soft laughter on the other end.

"Oh," he said knowingly. "One of *those* dreams."

I hurried to correct him. "No! Not one of those."

"Darn. I was hoping you were going to tell me about it."

"The next one I have, I promise you'll be the first to know."

"The first?"

"Whoops. The only one to know."

"So what did you dream about?"

"I had a visit from Vanessa Markham."

"The Vanessa Markham who was murdered?"

"That's the one. She sort of thanked me for finding her killer."

"That was kind of her."

"And then she said something about things we hide from each other. Oh, and she said I was fat."

"... Yeah. Hey Bets, I have to go. The storm's picking up and I need to concentrate. Talk to you later."

There's nothing like telling other people your dreams to get them to hang up the phone quickly, I thought. Still, though, I couldn't get Vanessa Markham's face out of my memory. She was a pain in life and it looked as if death hadn't changed her.

With the phone still in my hand, I decided to call Rocky and talk to him about my city council piece. Maybe talking to Rocky would wipe Vanessa out of my head.

"It's about time you called me," Rocky said a few minutes later.

"Yeah, I'm sorry I'm running a little late. I'm moving pretty slowly these days."

"Understandable."

"I have the city council grill-off piece finished. I can email it over to you in the next hour."

"So how was your experience interviewing the candidates? Get any good stuff?"

"Well, I collected a couple of recipes, which is why you sent me on the interviews."

"Yes, I know, but we could use some better dirt to spice up this race. People are holed up inside their houses under the air conditioners, and once the hurricane blows through life in this town will go back to boring. I have to fill up a newspaper, you know."

"I know."

"So, what did you pick up on with these two guys? Who was more helpful? Who did you like more? Anything we can use to pit one against the other? Give me the scoop."

I debated what to say. I could tell him about seeing Digby at the motel, or I could keep it to myself. Maybe he already knew about Digby and was just trying to see if I knew?

"That Digby fellow is as slippery as they come," he said. That was it. He did know. In a town this small, an affair would be difficult to hide.

"So you know?"

"Uh, you're going to have to be more specific."

"You know? About Baxter Digby?"

Rocky paused for a moment and then continued. "Of course. Just tell me what you know, and I'll tell you what I know."

"Come off of it, Rocky. Either you know or you don't."

"You first."

I was beginning to think Rocky didn't know anything about Baxter Digby and the motel. He was just trying to trick me into saying it.

"Now you have to tell me," Rocky said.

"No, I don't."

"Yes, you do. You're sitting on top of something about Digby."

I sighed, giving in to him. "I'm probably jumping to conclusions, but I've seen his car at the Super Stay Motel twice in the last two days, right at lunch time."

I could hear Rocky's chair squeak as he leaned back. "Isn't this interesting? Did you see anybody with him?"

"Rocky, I didn't even see him. I only saw his car."

"That's good enough for me." Waves of guilt started washing over me. What if Rocky ran with this and embarrassed Baxter Digby, or worse, embarrassed his wife? I should've kept quiet about it.

"You have to promise me that even if you find out he is having an affair, you don't put it in the newspaper."

"I don't have to promise anything. News is news, and you should know that by now."

"Rocky. A story like this could destroy a man's life. Have you thought of that?"

"And do we want a morally corrupt politician in city council? Wait—let me rephrase that. Do we want *another* morally corrupt politician in city council?"

Sometimes all Rocky could see of the world was black-and-white newsprint, and this was one of those occasions. "Okay, now that I've blurted out what is probably wrong, I can see I'm going to have to prove to you that Baxter Digby is not having an affair."

"That would just about do it."

"Then that's what I'm going to do. If you put this in the paper, I will never forgive myself."

"Then you'd better invest in a therapist, darlin'," he said as he hung up the phone.

I sent off my article wishing I had never called. If Baxter Digby was having an affair, there was one predictable source that would know.

"Betsy," Ruby Green said as I entered The Best Little Hairhouse in Texas. She put down her movie magazine and came over, putting her arm around me. "Come on and put your feet up. Pearly? Get Betsy a cold drink."

I sat down on one of the chairs in the waiting area. Ruby wore a bright green smock and neon green capri pants. At her neck she wore a flame colored red and orange scarf, and her earrings were two red orange and black macaw parrots. Pearly returned with a can of soda.

"I know this much sugar is probably not good for the baby, but one little Coke isn't going to hurt you." Pearly smiled hunching her shoulders as she shared this little indulgence.

"Sure, a little bit can't hurt me." I had been so careful watching what I ate, especially if I didn't count my trips to Bennie's Barbecue. I gulped down the cool drink.

"There you go, honey, that will cool you down. Being pregnant in Texas in the summer is like being at the doorway to hell."

"I know what you mean. I can't wait for holidays like Christmas and Thanksgiving because I won't be pregnant anymore and the temperature will finally be below 90.

"So what brings you here today? Come to get your hair done before the delivery?"

I reached up and touched my brown curls, which had grown to shoulder length in the last year. "No, I just wondered if I could talk to you about something..." I paused and leaned closer to whisper in her ear. "...in private."

Ruby's artfully lined eyes widened. "Oh Betsy," she exclaimed. "Any time, darlin'. You know you're like a second daughter to me."

I looked around the crowded salon. All eyes were now upon me. I might as well have used a megaphone and announced my request up and down Main Street.

"Do you think we could go into your back room?"

Ruby put her hand at my elbow. "Of course." She helped me out of the chair and hustled us to her storage room, a small space with a stained sink and boxes of various kinds of beauty supplies. I started to ask my question about Baxter Digby, but paused when I heard footsteps coming near us.

Hearing them too, Ruby knocked on the door. "We hear you, ladies." I then heard the rustle of feet moving back into the salon. Ruby reached over and turned on the water, the splashing sounds filling the room.

"I saw this once in a spy movie," Ruby said. "Never thought I'd actually find myself ducking in a storage room to pass secret messages." She giggled. "What's up?"

"I was just wondering if you have ever heard anything about somebody having an affair here in town."

"Well, I hear all kinds of stories around here. That doesn't mean any of them are true." Ruby jumped. "Oh no! Are you saying you think Leo is having an affair?"

"No. No it's not Leo. It's somebody else."

She pursed her lips and furrowed her brow. "Is it you?" she asked in a hushed voice.

"No."

"Because if you were, in your condition, I would be totally re-evaluating my opinion of you. So, Leo's not having an affair, and you're not having an affair and yet you want to talk about somebody doin' the hootchy coochy. Can you at least give me some clues?"

"Baxter Digby."

"Baxter Digby?" She asked as if it were the last name she expected to hear.

"I've seen Baxter Digby's car in front of the Super Stay Motel for two days in a row. I stupidly said something to Rocky about it, and maybe there's nothing going on, you know?"

"Sure."

"... And now Rocky is determined to prove that Baxter Digby is having an affair. I can't let him do that. I never should've said anything. Now I feel like I have to prove that Baxter Digby was at the hotel for some other reason."

"And what reason would that be?" Ruby asked.

"I don't know, but I thought if he was having an affair you might know who he would be with."

"Well, I thank you for your faith in me, but believe it or not I don't know everything that goes on in this town. The best thing I can tell you to do is to wait outside the Super Stay and see who is going into that room. Then you'll have your answer. Oh, and when you do find out, come on back here and tell me about it. On the QT of course."

CHAPTER 11

"According to these directions, there should be something right here to steady it," I said.

I sat in the nursery holding the instructions that came with the changing table, which was now partially assembled, but listing to the left.

My dad sat underneath the table, armed with a screwdriver and losing his patience. Try as we may, our table looked nothing like the diagram on the instruction sheet.

"Do these people on the other side of the world not know how to build things, or do they just not know how to explain things?"

He sat up abruptly, nearly hitting his head.

"Let me see that damn diagram again."

I handed my father the folded set of instructions which he rattled open. He adjusted his glasses down to the end of his nose.

"Hmmm... just what I thought."

"What's that?"

"These directions are written for idiots by idiots."

"Well then I guess we qualify."

"I'm just going to try to visualize this," he said, putting down the instructions.

"My daddy put together furniture all the time, and he didn't need directions in four different languages to do it. Back in those days if you wanted a changing table you went and bought some wood—or even better, you started from scratch and chopped down a tree."

"That must've been before fiberboard trees were planted."

"Damn straight." He tried turning the instructions upside down to see if that made more sense.

"I think I figured it out, Betsy."

It was great to know that the Pecan Bayou's master detective had solved the mystery of assembling a mail order changing table. He angled the changing table slightly and stuck some cardboard under it to steady it.

"Just one more problem."

"And that is?"

"We're missing a piece."

"No! Really? This can't be happening."

"This is what happens when you order things off the Internet."

"Is there anything we can do to replace it?" I asked.

"Sure. Call the manufacturer and have them send you another changing table."

"Sure and by the time they ship it, the baby will be here." I let out a frustrated sigh.

"Well then you'll just have to change him or her on the bed until you get this put together. You know you could always drive into the city and buy a changing table. You don't have to order everything off the computer."

"You're probably right. But I really liked the color of this one. If Leo doesn't want me driving to camp to pick up the boys, going to Houston is out of the question."

"Right. I'm sorry. I wasn't thinking. You don't need to be making any car trips in your condition. Maybe I could do it."

"Even if you wanted to make a trip for me, you really don't have time either between hurricane prep and the robberies we're having."

"You mean the midnight rustler?"

"Is that what you're calling him?"

"Not yet, but I'm sure Rocky will come up with a name for the guy. This is the most bizarre thing that ever happened around these parts."

"Do you have any idea who might be behind it?" I asked.

"You know, FBI profilers just don't have much on people who steal giant replicas of animals. Go figure."

"Seems a shame. So do you think it's somebody here in town or could it be the proverbial drifter?"

"Now there's an idea," my dad said. "The guy steals a cow and then jumps a freight train? Not likely."

"There is one positive side to all of this. If we do get a hurricane, that's two creatures that won't be blowing around in the wind causing damage."

In a hurricane force wind a trash can lid can decapitate someone. The damage a flying horse could do to a person would be devastating.

"True."

From downstairs I heard the front door open and close.

"Betsy? I'm home. Any babies yet?" I heard Leo's keys drop into the bowl next to the door.

"Not yet," I yelled.

"But she does have a grumpy old man trying to put together a changing table," my dad chimed in. "Maybe you can figure it out."

Leo bounded up the stairs. After the long day he had put in, his energy was amazing.

"Looks like it's mostly together," Leo said, observing our efforts.

"Not quite," My father said as he slapped the crumpled instruction sheet into Leo's hands.

"Figure that out, college boy."

Leo examined the directions, and then walked over to the crooked piece of furniture we were calling a changing table. He started hemming and hawing enough to make Bob Vila proud. He walked completely around the changing table, running his hand along the top rail.

"Looks like there's a piece missing."

"What was your first clue, Sherlock?" My father cracked.

Leo then picked up the empty box and turned it upside down. The missing leg fell onto the carpet.

"Damn. Didn't think to check the box," my father said.

"Not a problem." Leo grinned. "I'm here to serve."

"So what's this I hear about my son-in-law and soon to be the father of my grandchild flying off into a hurricane and leaving my darling daughter back here alone?"

The sheepish look on Leo's face said it all. "I know it looks bad on the surface, but it really was the opportunity of a lifetime. I went up with the 53rd Air Force squadron. You should know it was perfectly safe and I was never in danger. We gauged the wind speed and how quickly the hurricane will be coming to shore."

"Shoot, son. I think I would have had a hard time passing up a chance to fly with the Air Force."

Leo nodded as they shared a testosterone fueled moment. I scowled at my father. Nothing like encouraging Leo to risk his life.

"I'm just glad I was able to do it, and Betsy didn't go into labor."

"That was cutting it pretty close. Betsy has been in labor by herself once before. I sure would hate to see that happen again."

I could see Leo was feeling guilty, especially after my mentioning that the father of my last child hadn't been there for me either.

"Don't worry about it, Leo," I assured him. "You managed to get there and back in one day and everything was fine here."

"Except the cow being stolen," Leo said, looking to my father with a grin.

My father shook his head in annoyance. "Oh, yes. The crime wave continues. I'm sure when you moved to this town you never thought you'd be in a bed of petty theft."

"Really. I think I was safer in Dallas."

"I'm just glad you're back and now we can concentrate on having the baby," I said. "No more wild trips, right?"

Leo's lips thinned a bit. "Uh..."

"No!" I cut him off.

"No," he repeated.

"Listen to me son," my dad said, "whatever happens with the hurricane, just know when it comes to Betsy here, I'll step in whenever I can."

"I know Judd, and I'm really thankful for that," Leo said. My dad, looking a little overwhelmed by Leo's honest admission of gratefulness, cleared his throat.

"And how is my grandbaby doing?"

"Flying around in his own hurricane down there," I answered, feeling the baby shift.

"Oh, so it is a boy. I knew it! I just knew it."

"Don't get so excited. Just because I used the word 'him' it doesn't necessarily mean it's a boy."

"So it's a girl?"

"Didn't say that either. You'll find out when you find out."

"I see."

Leo patted my dad on the back. "That's okay Judd. We're all anxious to meet this new little Fitzpatrick."

"That's Kelsey-Fitzpatrick," my dad said as he put on his hat. "If the kid has all those names to write on his paper, you'd better name him Joe. At this rate he'll never get out of the second grade."

CHAPTER 12

The next morning I sat at the kitchen table with Aunt Maggie, drinking coffee and pre-addressing birth announcements. Once the baby came, I would fill in the details, but we could get a head start on the job now. Danny was in the den watching cartoons.

Maggie pulled the latest edition of the Gazette off the counter. "Looks like nothing was stolen overnight. Guess our burglar must be slowing down."

"To be honest there's not much left in town for him to steal."

"It's just downright weird. You know if I felt desperate enough to steal something, it would be something that would help me or my family."

"Which makes you wonder about the mental state of the thief. Have you noticed anyone crazy walking around?"

"How long have you got?"

"Point made. Hey Maggie, can I ask you something?"

Aunt Maggie, who had been putting stamps on envelopes, stopped and looked up.

"Sure, baby, anything. What do you need to know?"

"Have you heard anything about Baxter Digby?"

"You mean like he cheated someone on a house deal or something?" She clucked and shook her head. "Not surprising."

"No. Nothing like that. What do you know about his marriage?" Aunt Maggie's eyebrows shot up. She set the birth announcements aside.

"What are you trying to say?"

I was doing a lousy job of keeping a secret. Ruby knew and of course, Rocky knew. I foolishly thought I could get it by Rocky by asking a simple question. Giving Rocky a clue about a possible scandal was like advertising a shoe sale at a depression convention.

Maggie sat back and crossed her arms. "Spill it. What do you know?"

"I was interviewing him for this crazy article Rocky has me writing, and I found out something."

Maggie stared at me for moment, her eyes boring into mine, making me feel like she had caught me doing something bad. I felt like I was eight years old again. If Baxter Digby was going to have any privacy, I needed to shut up. "It's nothing."

"So, that's your story and you're sticking to it."

"Yes."

"As far as Baxter Digby goes, I wouldn't trust him as far as I could throw him. He's a handsome fellow, and I think all that hair is really his, but there's just something about the guy. Did you know he forbade his wife to work outside the home? He said she's happier not working."

"Maybe she is."

"And good for her if it's true, but Ruby said he was bragging about it one day at a chamber of commerce meeting. Well maybe not bragging, as much as implying his family life is being better than households with two working parents."

"That's pretty archaic. I thought women being forced to stay home went out with the advent of women's lib."

"You never know about a man, and Digby strikes me as being pretty controlling. I heard he has quite the jealous streak."

"It doesn't exactly jive with what I'm suspecting. I think he might be cheating on his wife."

"Boy howdy. Now that's some hot gossip for sure."

"Yeah, but if he's so gung-ho about having a traditional family, why would he be sleeping around on his wife?"

"Because he calls the shots, baby girl. There's a reason why he's such a successful real estate agent. By controlling every variable he makes sure things go his way. I'll tell you one thing. Whoever he might be sleeping with probably has no idea what type of man he is. If he makes his wife stay home and not work, what does he demand of his mistress?"

"I'm being silly," I said. "I just saw his car parked outside a motel for two days in a row around lunchtime."

"Uh huh. How do you know it was his car?"

"I saw his bumper sticker on the back. 'You can bet on change with Baxter Digby.'"

"You'd think he would cover it up." Maggie smiled.

"I guess in his mind, any opportunity to promote himself is a good."

"Speaking of cars, I noticed Leo's car isn't in the driveway. He must've gone in early."

"Very early. He's catching up after taking time out yesterday to go flying into the hurricane."

"I heard. Doesn't he know you're about to have a baby?"

"He does, and I'm just glad he's back on the ground. No more death-defying weather measurements."

"Let's hope," Maggie said. "Why doesn't he just take up walking on top of moving trains, or maybe when the circus comes in town, he can put his head in the lion's mouth."

"I know. Still though, I just had to let him go. I can't go stomping on his dream."

"You have more patience than I do."

The baby shifted. I moved slightly to accommodate his new position.

"Is the baby moving?" Maggie asked.

"Yes. He's quite active these days." Aunt Maggie reached over and rested her hand on my belly. After a few seconds the baby moved again.

"Oh. I felt it." Aunt Maggie's eyes glistened. "This is wonderful. I really felt it. I just can't wait to see this baby. Are you all packed and ready?"

"Yes, mostly. I just have to put a phone charger in my bag."

"Well you'd better get it packed, because this little fella is itching to come out."

"You know, I'm getting that feeling too."

"Have you started dilating?" This intimate information was something mothers and mothers-to-be always exchanged at this point. It wasn't exactly a question to ask in mixed company, but still it was an important foretelling of the baby's arrival.

"Not yet."

"I'm just hoping this baby isn't born during the storm. Does the storm have an official name yet?"

"I heard it was Ezra."

"I guess that's fitting. If it's a boy you can call him Ezra, and if it's a girl you can call her Esther." Maggie grinned.

"Hope you don't mind me passing on that suggestion. I was watching the forecast the other day, and Hurricane Hal has two charts up on it in NUTV. One to track the incoming hurricane and one to predict the arrival of my baby."

Aunt Maggie laughed. "You have to be kidding me."

"Yes, and then I heard about a betting pool going down over at Bubba's Beer and Bait."

"Who told you that?"

"Dad. He put a ten spot on next Thursday."

"It hardly seems fair. He has insider information."

"Whatever. I'll just be happy for the hurricane to be over and my baby to come into the world safe and sound."

"Do you ever worry about Down Syndrome? What with Danny and all?"

"No. Not really. I have to admit the thought has crossed my mind here and there, but watching you and Danny all of these years has taken a lot of the fear of the unknown away for me. Danny isn't like other men, but he's Danny. He's a wonderful, loving, sweet cousin and friend. I wouldn't want him any other way. One time Zach asked Pastor Green what Danny would be like in Heaven. The reverend told him just like he is now, because he's already perfect."

"He's right." Danny said from the other room. "I'm already perfect."

"Oh my." Aunt Maggie reached for the handkerchief in her purse and with a snort said, "Enough of that now. It's not hard to make an old lady cry, you know."

"You're right," I said, wiping a tear out of my own eye.

"Have we addressed enough cards for everyone on the list?" Maggie asked.

"I think so, unless somebody moves into town in the next week."

"Are you hungry? I think Danny and I will head over to Birdie's for a cinnamon roll. Can I get you one?"

"No, thank you. Better not."

"Good girl. Somewhere along the line you go from baby weight to ten extra pounds and nowhere to put it." She patted me on the shoulder as she rose to go.

What she didn't know was I was already thinking about picking up my piece of pie over at Benny's. Yes, I could do with some pie.

CHAPTER 13

An hour later I waited at the takeout counter at Benny's Barbecue. I was a little later than my normal time, and the lunch rush was in full swing. Benny was ringing sales up on the register, while his father was manning the kitchen in the back.

Benny pulled my bag out from under the counter. "Here you go, Betsy. Enjoy."

"Thank you." I grabbed my bag and looked around for Benny's new waitress.

"Where's Sasha today?" I asked.

"Oh, um... she took a lunch break."

"You give lunch breaks at a place that serves lunch?"

"Yeah, I know it's silly, but she goes out right around noon every day to check on her mother. Her mom needs help with her noon meal, and it just worked out for her."

Benny really was too nice of a guy. He had been Zach's scout leader and served as a positive male role model in Zach's life when I was a single mom. Zach also spent time with Benny's three boys, which prepared Zach for having a brother of his own in Tyler.

"What does Celia think of the help leaving during the lunch hour?"

"My wife doesn't know much about Sasha's lunch runs yet. As a matter fact it might be a good idea not to mention it at all. We wouldn't want to worry her."

Celia had a reputation for running a tight ship at the restaurant.

The door behind me jangled as more hungry customers filed in behind me. Benny glanced at his watch. I felt sorry for the guy. I picked up my bag to go.

"How much longer?" he asked.

"About two weeks."

"Well, I guess it couldn't last forever. I was hoping your cravings would help me finance a new wing on the restaurant, or at least hire another waitress. Oh, and by the way, I put twenty dollars down over at Bubba's Beer and Bait betting you have the baby during the hurricane."

"That is, if you know when the hurricane is going to hit."

"I figured I could just ask your significant other. He ought to know."

"Leo went up with the Air Force yesterday to watch them take some measurements."

"Boy howdy. Sounds dangerous."

"I know, but he's on the ground now, and his hazardous storm chasing is over."

"You must be relieved. If I had done something like that when Celia was pregnant there would have been hell to pay. And not just from her, but from her mama. You don't want to cross my mother-in-law if you plan to live to tell about it."

I laughed and waved goodbye as I made room for the next customer in line.

As I drove back home, I couldn't help myself. I slowed down in front of the Super Stay Motel to scope out the parking lot. Sure enough, there sat Baxter Digby's car, with the now familiar blue Subaru next to it.

As interesting as this was, I was more alarmed by what I saw across the street from the motel. Rocky sat in his green pickup, camouflaged by a row of bushes. He was trying to catch Digby.

I parked and walked over Rocky's truck and tapped on the window. His air conditioner was running full blast and Willie Nelson blared on the radio. Rocky jumped. The window buzzed as he it rolled down.

"Rocky! What are you doing?"

"And how are you today Miss Betsy? I see you're still in the family way."

"I was doing pretty well until I drove down the street and found you spying on Baxter Digby."

"Like I always say, news is news."

"Rocky!" I scolded, reaching for the camera in his hand. He pulled it away and readjusted the camera's focus on the motel. I looked around, opened the door, and climbed into the cab with him.

"So have you seen anything?"

"Maybe."

"What you mean?"

"Whoever our Salesman of the Year is meeting at this motel was already here when he arrived. I'm guessing our lady friend is the owner of the blue Subaru you see there. From the looks of the paint job, whoever might be driving it is pretty down on her luck."

Rocky straightened as the motel door opened and Baxter Digby stepped out. A woman reached out and grabbed him around the neck, pulling him back into the room. They kissed. As his arms went around her, she came out onto the sidewalk, dressed only in a towel.

It was easy to identify the mystery woman as Sasha Holman from Benny's. And it was clearly not her elderly mother she was taking care of. Rocky started clicking off pictures as fast as he could.

I turned to Rocky.

"You can't use those pictures."

"Why not?"

"Because it will ruin this man's career."

"Betsy, I think you're a little mixed up. The person who is ruining Baxter Digby's career is Baxter Digby. If he can't control his impulses with a woman other than his wife, what's he going to do once he gets in office? What about when he gets his hands on Pecan Bayou's city funds? Why, he could be spending our money on a whole group of mistresses. We'll have to put in a new motel chain just to meet his needs."

I was amazed at how quickly Rocky's mind went from fact to fiction.

"You just cannot use those pictures. I know Digby isn't the nicest man in town, but he still deserves to know he's been caught cheating before reading about it in the paper."

Rocky wasn't accustomed to being challenged on his editorial decisions. I could tell he was losing his temper.

"Listen to me, young lady. I've been doing this for years around here. I'm what you might call the voice of the people. You know I would never do anything to hurt a person on purpose. Right?"

I thought about all the times he had printed stuff about me and my father. I started to answer honestly, but he cut me off.

"...So I will at least talk to Baxter Digby before I put these pictures in the paper. And what about the woman? Aren't you being a little sexist not worrying about me harming *her* professional life?"

"She's a waitress, and she's newly divorced."

"How do you know that?" Rocky asked.

"I just do."

"For a helpful hints columnist, you're pretty in-the-know. I promise you, before I print anything, I'll try to let Digby know."

"Well, how thoughtful of you. When will you be calling him? Will it be before or after the morning edition hits his front stoop?"

Rocky smiled. "I haven't decided." His response told me he would give Baxter Digby very little warning.

"You know, don't worry about it. I'll tell Baxter Digby."

I clambered out of his truck and headed back to my car. After buckling my seatbelt, I decided against confronting Diby in a motel room, with his mistress in a towel. I would go see Digby after a little rest.

CHAPTER 14

Back home and digging into my afternoon pie, I thought about Baxter Digby and Sasha Holman. What was it that made men in political office unable to control their sexual urges? Did Sasha know she had traded a smiley face painter to a jealous, obsessive manipulator?

I ate half the piece of pie and set down my fork. Relaxing in the rocking chair, I was hoping for another dream. Dreaming about dead people was weird, but it fascinated me.

I found myself walking in a field of Texas bluebonnets mixed in with a swath of burnt orange Indian paintbrushes. The birds were singing, and I could feel the warmth of the sun on my skin. I felt the same giddiness I always experience in springtime, the air warm enough but not too warm. I felt my soul being renewed as I shook off all the heat and weight of my long pregnant summer. Water rushed in the distance, the sound playing on my ears.

As I moved closer to the sound, the tinkling began to morph from a gentle rhythm of cascading water to an irritating buzz. The smell of the flowers came up into my nostrils, almost overpowering me with a sweet cloying scent. The bee boxes from Stokes Flower Farm stood in a line like little square tanks filled with buzzing soldiers.

Suddenly, beekeeper Lenny Stokes stepped out from behind a sweeping magnolia tree, dressed in his white wife-beater t-shirt and droopy khaki pants.

The last time I had seen Lenny, he was lying on the ground next to these same white bee boxes. At his death, his skin was mottled and swollen from hundreds of bee stings. Now the bites had disappeared, and he looked healthy and cleaner than I remembered him in real life. The bees grew quiet as Lenny made his way toward me. His upper lip curled to show a row of healthy pink gums absent of teeth.

"About time you showed up." A bee flew up from a box and rested on his bald head. While others might swat it away, he wasn't bothered by it.

"Sorry to keep you waiting."

He surveyed my belly. "I'm supposin' you have your reasons." Maybe he was a little kinder in the place he rested now than he had been in life.

"You wanted to speak with me?" Just like all the others, he had to have some kind of weird message for me.

"What are you blabbering about, girlie?"

"Trust me."

He reached up and removed the little bee from his forehead. He petted it gently with his index finger. "My life was never what I thought it would be."

The old man reached out and carefully replaced the bee into the buzzing box behind him. More bees flew out and landed on his arm. I counted ten, and then twenty, resting peacefully on his bony reach.

"I had everything with my Martha. It was all good, but then I turned angry. It was as if the right in my world cracked open and the bad came flying out. The boogey men. The shadow people. Things that can make a good man go bad."

"So, your message from the beyond is you feel bad about your life?" His gaze shifted from the bees to me.

"I know I should be saying thank you. You're a problem solver. You can't help yourself sometimes." True to form, he left me with an insult, as he started to fade out from me. "You always did have your nose in other people's business."

I woke with a gasp and choked, thinking a bee might have flown into my throat. As I became more awake, I realized there was no bee. My visit from Lenny was stranger than the other dreams. As I felt heat on the back of my neck, now damp, I remembered the refreshing spring air. Butch, alarmed at sudden movement, was now licking my hand.

"I'm okay, boy," I reassured him, petting him on the head.

Too bad I had to run into the beekeeper. I wished I could sprint across that field, skinny again, with Leo waiting for me to jump into his arms. We would make love in the bluebonnets with the warm sun shining down on us and the smell of the flowers encircling us. Instead, I run into a grumpy beekeeper who couldn't even thank me without insulting me.

I grabbed my trash and went downstairs to turn on the television. Hurricane Ezra was spinning on the screen, and computer models indicated it was headed right for Houston. I called Leo.

"Hey, just checking in. I saw the hurricane on television."

"Are you having a baby? Do I need to come get you?"

"I'm fine."

He sighed. "Good. Ezra is incredible. I can't believe I was up in the middle of it. Thank you, thank you, thank you. They said next time they might let me go up again because I did such a good job."

I know I should have congratulated him at this point, but the idea of him going up in these clouds on a regular basis was not something I could deal with at the moment.

"The Air Force guys, or the Hurricane Hunters as they like to be called, are a different breed of people. They're not afraid to do anything. They see a storm, and while everybody else would run away, they put on their backpacks and fly into it." Shades of Ghostbusters crossed my mind and I wasn't sure if my husband was channeling Bill Murray or Dan Akroyd.

"That's great." My answer was underwhelming.

"I met one guy named Nate who just called me. Not only does he go up in these flights to measure the wind speed, but on weekends he's a tornado hunter. Isn't it wild? He has his truck completely outfitted with equipment so he can record data on the tornadoes and get live footage. These are the pioneers of weather. It's like I was hanging out with Ford or Edison. These guys are on top of it all. They don't look at weather through a computer; they look at it through their binoculars. They live it!"

Leo had converted to the ranks of daredevil weather chasers. I felt stranded in the eye of a hurricane.

"Now that we have a storm, and we know that it's Houston, what's our emergency plan?" I asked. Leo didn't immediately respond, as if he hadn't considered how it would affect his own family. I don't know if I found that amazing or downright scary.

He finally spoke up. "We need to make sure that we have our hurricane supplies on hand. You know—water, non-perishable food, and batteries. Find the weather radio and put the flashlights in places you can find in the dark." I already had most of those supplies in a shed or the garage labeled emergency supplies.

"Do you think we should go get the boys?" I asked.

"Looking at the path of the storm, unless it veers in the direction of the camp when it comes on land, they're probably safer there."

"Unless?"

"Weather is more predictable than ever, but it's too early to predict what it will do after it makes landfall. We'll know more as the storm gets closer to land."

"Will that give us time to get the boys evacuated?"

"I wish I could give you a better answer, but I just can't."

"If we do have to rescue them, how do we get them? You can't leave your job. My dad can't leave his. I suppose we could send Aunt Maggie."

"Haven't you told me over and over how frightened Danny is of bad storms? She certainly couldn't leave him here alone. If he gets way out of sorts, I don't know if we could handle him."

"So, what do we do?"

"I need to think about this. Sorry Bets, I really have to go. I need to call my mother to make sure she's planning to leave Galveston. Sometimes she gets that 'hunker down' mentality when it comes to her house." Gwyn's two story house fronted the water. It was her own personal paradise. Leaving it would be tough for anyone.

I closed out my call with Leo. Hurricane Hal still chattered on TV.

"You heard it right folks. We have a big one heading right for us. Better get down to your favorite store and pick up bottled water and all your essentials before they're gone. Oh, and for those of you planning your storm party, Bubba's Beer and Bait will be selling beer by the caseload out the back door." Storm party. Only in Pecan Bayou would this make the weather forecast.

"And if things get dicey, we just want you to know the city council is setting up an emergency shelter in the Nolan Ryan Middle School gymnasium. If you find you are in the path of the storm and told to evacuate, head on over to the school. Oh, and PTA president Phyllis Hamlin stresses that none of Bubba's Beer will be let into the building. You'll have to tailgate just like you do at the games. Also for all the travelers from out of town, we will be providing shelter for them in the LBJ high school gym. They don't need to know they're getting the older facility. Ain't that right folks?"

As I listened to Hurricane Hal— or Hurricane Hell as my father loved to call him—I began to feel like time was running out. The waiting was ending. The hurricane was coming, and I was nearing the beginning of labor. I would go crazy if I spent any more time in my house.

My mind raced as I fought off a case of worry overload. I tried rationalizing my fears. What was there to worry about? Leo chasing storms? The boys in danger at summer camp? Hurricane Ezra triggering storms on land or—oh yeah, the birth of my baby?

It was just too much for me to think about. I longed for the days when all I did was write my helpful hints column and solved a few murders. Whatever happened to those carefree days? I knew what I needed to do. I would work on the thefts of the animals. In my physical state it would be a harmless way to occupy my brain. I grabbed a notebook and pencil out of the kitchen drawer, and started writing down everything I knew about the two thefts.

First there was Charlie Loper's horse. There weren't that many Charlie Loper fans left, but maybe an overeager octogenarian wanted it for his personal collection. It was probably standing right next to Howdy Doody's red bandana and Captain Kangaroo's ping pong balls. An eighty-year-old who could move a life-size horse? Still, it was a motive. I wrote it down.

Then we had the big brown cow outside the Cattleman's Call. This thief had to be the same person who stole Charlie's horse because, come on, how often are there two wackos running around stealing display animals? If it was the same person, the idea of it being the world's oldest cowboy fan becomes less plausible. That cow never had a minute of screen time as far as I knew. So now this person had a horse and cow hidden off somewhere. What could being going on in the mind of the thief? I sat back in my chair feeling the baby shift from one side to the other. Could it be my future offspring enjoyed solving mysteries?

I was beginning to feel some heartburn. At this point, eating anything greasy like fried chicken gave me some intense stomach distress. Having the baby crowding all the organs that might aid in digesting the grease wasn't helping matters. No greasy chicken, or chicken fried steak, or breaded pork chops. Just about anything on Birdie's menu could send me to the medicine cabinet for antacid.

That was when it hit me. There was now a giant chicken on the roof of Birdie's Diner made out of soup cans. The chicken had to be the next victim of the critter-stealing thief. This was just what I needed to get my mind off my worries. I would stake out Birdie's Diner. However, I realized if I were going to do this, I would need to take precautions, being this close to delivery. I had done my share of sleuthing over the years, but this was the first time I was investigating for two. I phoned Aunt Maggie.

"Is it time?" She answered. Damn that caller ID. Couldn't I call anybody on the phone without them thinking I was in the final stages of labor?

"No. I'm fine. I was wondering if you could help me out with something tonight."

"Anything. Just ask."

"Great. Will you sit with me while I do surveillance on Birdie's Diner tonight?"

"Are you sure you're not in labor?"

"Yes! I mean no. I am not having a baby. Maybe I need to call NUTV and have them broadcast it. I am not having a baby today."

"No need to call. They're already running daily bulletins. Seriously, listen to yourself. You want to go and sit outside Birdie's tonight? You are having a baby. People who have babies do not sit in cars all night."

"They do when they're going crazy sitting around the house worrying about a hurricane."

"And this is your solution to reducing anxiety? I think this pregnancy is going to your head."

"Please, Aunt Maggie?" I begged. She didn't answer me. I knew I was close to winning.

"What am I supposed to do with Danny?"

"Bring him along. It'll be fun. Like when we used to go to the drive-in."

"I suppose he could bring his blanket and his pillow and sleep in the back seat." Score one for Betsy. We were going to catch a thief.

CHAPTER 15

By nine o'clock we were parked in an inconspicuous spot across the street from Birdie's Diner. I nibbled on one of Aunt Maggie's biscuits to take my mind off my aching back. When Maggie handed me a piece of chicken, I waved her off.

"I just thought fried chicken would be appropriate for a stakeout of Birdie's Diner," Maggie said.

"It is perfect," I said, "but I don't think I can handle it right now." I shifted in my seat.

"More for me," Danny said from the back seat.

We stared up at the roof of Birdie's Diner. Birdie had closed the diner half an hour ago and the setting sun backlit the large metal chicken on the roof. Birdie's boyfriend had spray painted the hobbled-together bird and it did resemble a chicken, somewhat. The glow from the setting sun made the big bird look more like the victim of a nuclear accident near a chicken farm than a family restaurant mascot.

"Now what is it that makes you think the serial animal thief will be coming for the soup-can chicken tonight?" Maggie asked.

"The hurricane. Super chicken over there doesn't stand a chance in this storm. Our thief will want to add it to his herd and get it under wraps before the storm hits. While most people are buying bottled water, this guy is stocking up on fake animals. Makes sense to me."

"Me too," Danny said, his mouth full of biscuit. "Did you pack the lemonade too?"

Maggie pulled out her thermos of fresh lemonade. She poured Danny a cup and passed it back to him.

"Thanks Mama," he said. I picked up the binoculars and scanned the front of the restaurant.

"Have you tried Birdie's new pecan crusted chicken?" Maggie said. "It's delicious and a great way to use up pecans."

"Not yet. Leo and I will have to try it next time we're out with the boys."

"And the baby." Maggie smiled.

"Yes. We'll have the baby, too."

I glanced back up at the chicken. It was still holding down the roof. I still hadn't had time to ask Birdie about her new boyfriend. She had been single for as long as I could remember. I thought it was strange she had a boyfriend that none of us had met. Whoever this man was he was artistic enough to make a giant chicken. What else could he do?

"Do you see anything yet?" Danny whispered as if the thief would hear us.

"Not yet."

"Will the guy be wearing a black mask?"

"Why would you think that, Danny?" I asked.

"Because the bad guy always wears a black mask in the cartoons. There are holes cut out in the middle for his eyes, so he can see where he's going. Seems like the cops would see those masks and know right away who the bad guy was."

"If it were only that easy, your uncle Judd would be able to go fishing more often," Maggie said.

"Don't you worry," Danny said,"if the bad guys show up, I brought my own mask." He pulled a black plastic mask out of his backpack and began slipping the elastic band over his ears. "I'm Batman. I get the bad guys." He removed the mask and looked at Maggie. "Did you bring the chocolate cake, too?"

Aunt Maggie reached down for her container of chocolate cake. She opened it with the precision of a surgeon and extracted a piece of cake, placing it on a napkin for Danny.

"Now don't you go making a mess in the back of Betsy's car. Betsy doesn't want to be scrubbing chocolate off the seat."

"Is this where you're going to have a baby? Right here in this very seat?"

"I hope not."

"I made a present for the baby."

"I know. I can't wait to see it."

"I can't wait to see the baby," he said.

I remembered when Zach was younger, he and Danny sat in front of the TV for hours watching cartoons. Danny and Zach played together for years, but now that Zach was getting older, Danny was losing his best buddy. I hoped this child would be as good a friend to Danny as Zach had been.

The street was eerily quiet on this hot summer night. Not a car or person in sight. Most people were inside with their air conditioners running, either asleep or watching television. After the food had been put away, we sat in the dark for what felt like forever.

"I don't know, Betsy. Maybe you were wrong about the thief."

"I'm sleepy. I want to go home and go to bed." Danny let out a huge yawn.

"I'm getting pretty tired myself. Maybe it is time for bed." Aunt Maggie said.

I felt sure the thief would hit tonight, so I really didn't want to leave. "Can we just wait another half hour?"

"I suppose," Aunt Maggie said, now settling comfortably in her seat. The ache in my back spread. I struggled to find a more comfortable position. I was so tired, my shoulders hurt.

I was convinced the thief would hit the chicken place. This was the only place left in town sporting an over-sized animal. It just had to be Birdie's and this had to be the night.

"You know you're just wasting your time, Betsy." I looked in the back seat, expecting to see Danny, but instead, Hunter Grayson, Libby Loper's dead butler, sat there examining his manicure.

"My, my. What a tacky car. When was the last time you sanitized back here?" he asked, pursing his lips and cocking his head sideways.

"So I must be dreaming again."

"What do you think?" His British accent, dripping with disapproval, put me in my place. I chose to ignore his condescending tone.

"What are you doing here?"

"You Americans. Always in such a hurry. Why do you suppose we're all being dragged out from The Great Beyond? Really, dearie, you may have solved my murder—and by the way, thank you for using your Yankee ingenuity on that—but still there does seem to be a recurring theme here."

"So do you have a message for me?" I knew these little meetings were brief, so there was no time for idle chit-chat.

"Did you enjoy going through all my treasures? Stupid Libby had no idea I was financing my dreams one gold card at a time."

"Your extensive vase collection struck me as a bit odd."

"I knew you were incapable of appreciating my fascination for them. They're so precious and breakable, but they're beautiful. I guess that's why I liked them so much. Once broken, a thing of beauty is gone forever. Crack. Your dream has vanished." He laughed at his own joke, although the humor was lost on me. His laughter changed into a knocking sound.

"Betsy? Is that you in there?" My father was tapping on the window. Maggie and Danny both jolted upright from their sleeping positions. I unrolled the window.

"Hey, Dad."

"Hi Uncle Judd," Danny chimed from the back seat.

"Hi Danny. And what are we all doing here tonight?" He directed his question toward Danny because he knew Danny would give his uncle a better answer than I would.

"I'm Batman. We are searching for bad guys."

"You are? Well that's just wonderful. See anything?"

Danny kept talking. "Yeah. I brought my bat signal just in case I had to signal you." He pulled out a little flashlight and turned it on. The light streamed through a bat cutout, projecting the image of a bat on my glove compartment.

"Impressive. We need one of those things down at the department."

Judd leaned on the door. "So are you three going to tell me what you're really doing, or should I arrest you for loitering?"

"It was Betsy's idea," Maggie said.

"Okay," I conceded, "I'll tell you why we're here. I think the chicken on the roof of Bird..." Before I could get the sentence out of my mouth, I realized the soup-can chicken was gone. It had been swiped while we were sleeping.

"Oh my," Aunt Maggie said, holding her head as if she were getting a headache.

"The chicken!" Danny said. "The bad guy stole the chicken!" My father turned around and looked toward the roof of Birdie's Diner.

"Looks like it, and you guys slept through it all. I guess we got ourselves another crime scene."

My dad walked over to his car radio. I knew he was calling Birdie to tell her she was another victim of our thief.

He returned with a flashlight. "I'm just going to search the back alley. You stay here."

"Why wouldn't I?" I said, batting my eyelashes.

"Smart ass." He walked off behind the diner.

I pulled myself out of the car.

"Danny can I use your Bat Signal?" I asked.

"Sure. Are you going to get the bad guy with my bat signal?"

"I'm going to try."

I turned on the flashlight, and the illuminated bat bounced on the side of the building as I walked. I could see a couple of spots of ripped roof shingle where I guessed that a ladder had been resting up against it. I noticed a tear in the awning on the front of the diner. Also from a ladder, was my guess.

I considered standing on the air conditioning unit to get a better look at the crime scene, but with Maggie watching, I thought better of it. I caught a whiff of the lingering odor of paint, triggering memories of art class in high school. I touched the wall to see if it was freshly painted, but my hand slid over a smooth dry surface.

"Betsy you be careful over there," Aunt Maggie said, worry creeping into her voice.

I knew I couldn't get up on the roof, so I circled the perimeter of the restaurant looking for clues. Maybe there were footprints, and if there were, I was stepping all over them. The light bounced on something scrawled on the wall. It might be graffiti, although I hadn't seen anything like that anywhere else in town. I brought the light closer and could see a circle with something inside.

A thief who liked big animals and smelled of paint—that could be anyone in Pecan Bayou. Around here, art in Pecan Bayou often consisted of paint-by-number specials bought at Super Walley. Holding the light closer to the wall, a yellow figure came into view. It was a smiley face. I knew who the thief was.

I flicked off the flashlight and hurried back to the car where Aunt Maggie and Danny waited.

"Did you see the bad man, Betsy?"

"Nope. He got away."

"Don't worry. Uncle Judd will get him. He always gets the bad men."

"That's right honey," Aunt Maggie said, stifling a yawn.

Birdie pulled in front of the diner, her tires squealing.

"Birdie, I didn't expect you down here this quickly." My father looked from Birdie to a man who stood with his arm around her. "And this is?"

"Sorry, Judd. This is my boyfriend. Jeff Ellis."

Ellis looked up at the roof.

"Dagnabbit." He hit his ball cap on the leg of his jeans. "I knew it. I called the police department right after the cow was stolen. The guy told me they don't do protective patrols for inanimate objects."

"Normally, we don't," my dad replied. "Who did you talk to, exactly?"

"That big guy with the high voice."

"That would have been Officer Beckman."

"Right—that dude."

"Who would steal a chicken made out of soup cans? I mean, what would it be worth to anybody?" Birdie said.

Jeff withdrew his arm from around Birdie's shoulder and faced her.

"Are you saying my chicken wasn't worth stealing?"

Realizing her error, Birdie backpedaled. "I'm just so upset."

I couldn't be sure, but I thought I saw a little relief in Birdie's eyes. Bad gifts from new boyfriends could be hard to say no to.

Birdie and her boyfriend talked to my father for a few more minutes. I stepped back to the car where Maggie was waiting.

"Well I guess this evening is a bust," I said.

"These things happen. Let's head home to get some sleep. I think we're all tuckered out."

Maggie was right. Suddenly, I was incredibly exhausted. Not only that, but I hadn't called Leo in the last few hours. If he were to get home before me and find out I had been trying to catch a thief all night, there would be hell to pay.

I dropped Maggie and Danny off and headed straight home. As I let myself into the house, my phone started ringing.

"Hey Betsy, sorry I'm so late calling. I'm on my way home right now. How are you feeling?"

"Oh... fine. Just fine." Leo did not respond immediately. We were getting to the point where he knew when I was trying to hide something.

"Are you sure? You not feeling the twinges of any kind of labor are you?"

"No. The baby is fine."

"Good. I'm so glad to hear that. I'm proud of you for taking a night to relax. We have a big delivery coming, and you need all the energy you can get."

I had a pang of guilt as I remembered how close I had come to climbing up on the air conditioner earlier. Should I tell him the truth, or should I just let him find out about it later? I decided to save it for later.

"It's all about taking care of yourself," I said.

"You're so right. I'll be home soon."

CHAPTER 16

After a lousy night's sleep, and once Leo left for the day, I decided to head over to Benny's Barbecue to have a talk with Sasha.

Sasha Holman, the waitress at Benny's, had mentioned her ex was a painter. She also mentioned her disapproval of his signature smiley face.

Would this guy be stupid enough to steal something and leave behind a signature? Signing a piece of art work is one thing, but signing a theft seemed a little out there, even for creative types.

"Well now, if it isn't Betsy. My most frequent customer. Aren't you just a few hours too early?" said Benny as I waddled in to his place of business.

"It's never too early for a good day. Isn't that what you told the boys when you made them get up at sunrise on all of those scout trips?"

Benny's smile took on a smirk. "Good times. What can I do for you?"

"I was wondering if Sasha was in yet."

"She's in the back. I'll get her." A minute later Sasha came out wearing a kitchen apron, wiping her hands on a dishtowel. Her luscious blond hair, crammed into a netted kitchen cap, transformed her from sexy to haggard. I wondered what Baxter Digby would think of this version of Sasha.

"You wanted to see me?" She looked nervous. It was unusual for a customer to ask for her by name, even if it was a pie-craving pregnant woman.

"Yes. Sorry to bother you, but I had a quick question. Didn't you say your ex-husband was a painter of some sort?"

She laughed, relaxing a little. "He fancies himself a painter. Does that count?"

"Can you tell me what kind of portraits he painted? I was thinking about maybe having a mural painted on the baby's wall."

"Well, if you want a picture with a bunch of cows in a pasture, then he's your guy."

"He paints mostly outdoor scenes with animals? Does he paint on location, or does he use photographs?"

"If you want to see an example of his work you just need to go over to Cattleman's Call. He painted a mural for that Carello guy. I really thought when he started the job at the steakhouse, things would pick up for us. Maybe his idea of being a painter wasn't so crazy. But no, my ex-husband messes it all up again, ending his chance at any future employment."

"What?"

"He puts his freakin' smiley face right there in the corner of the painting. Just ridiculous. Mr. Carello was so angry. He told him to go back and paint over it. Connor wouldn't and said it was his artistic license. Hell, he even painted one on the back of my car. You can bet I scratched that sucker off. He said that smiley face was his unique signature. That explanation works if you're a sixth grade girl."

"Did he paint over it?"

"Eventually. I made him. We had rent to pay."

"Would you mind telling me your address? I'm just finishing up the nursery and I'd like to talk with your ex-husband."

"No problem at all." She pulled out her order pad and started scribbling down an address. She ripped it off with a flourish.

"There you go. I hope you hire him. He needs the money."

I was already starting to get some cravings and felt the baby moving. I rested my hand on my offspring for just a moment.

"Do you want me to get you some pie?"

"It's a little early for it," I admitted, not wanting to tell her I left the house without breakfast. The baby shifted again.

"Are you getting kicked?" The woman across the table from me looked fondly at my belly. "I wish it were me. I would love to be having a baby right now."

The irony was, I would love *not* to be having a baby right now. I couldn't wait to see my new baby, but I couldn't wait to see my old waistline. I dreamed of wearing something as simple as a belt.

"Yes it's a wonderful time. Leo and I are very excited."

"Oh, yeah." Sasha snapped her fingers and pointed at me. "I forgot Leo Fitzpatrick is your husband. You are one lucky girl. I loved it when he did the weather on NUTV every day. I almost never missed the five day forecast." She smiled and gazed up in the air as if having a brief fantasy about my husband. I stopped her imagining cold.

"I know about Baxter Digby." She jerked out of her dream as her face registered shock. I shouldn't have blurted it out, but I just couldn't help myself when she started thinking about another married man. My married man. She had been so kind to me just a minute before. Now she looked as if she wanted to shoot me, or at least give me the wrong kind of pie.

"I don't know what you're talking about." Of course, she would deny it. How could she let it out she was sleeping with a married city council candidate and still come off as the victim of a crazy ex-husband?

"I saw you."

"What do you mean you saw me?" Sweet Sasha Holman's demeanor was growing very icy. Something pretty hard to achieve in the heat of August.

"I saw you at the Super Stay Motel."

"I don't know what you hoped to accomplish here," she said, turning away from me, "but I am not going to stay here and listen to your lies. Baxter Digby and I are friends. What does it matter anyway? I'm single."

She started to leave and I put my hand on her arm.

"But he's married. I think we both know that."

She tried to pull away from my grasp, but then turned toward me. "In name only," she muttered. For a woman who was madly in love, she didn't look too happy. Her eyes met mine.

"So, what is it you want from me? Is it money? Because I don't have any. I spent all my money on my divorce. Why do you think I'm working in this barbecue joint? I go home at night and I can't get the smell out of my clothes."

Benny, who had returned to the kitchen and was now flouring a load of chicken, looked up briefly, his lips thinning. This would probably be Sasha's last lunch break.

"No. I don't want your money. You've completely misunderstood this. I'm not here to try to get something out of you. I'm here because I need to let you know that Rocky Whitson at the Pecan Bayou Gazette is on to you."

"How did he find out?"

I lowered my gaze as the guilt took over.

"Somebody told him?" Sasha asked.

"Sort of."

"Who? Whoever it is better put their affairs in order, because I'm going to kill them. Who would do such a hateful thing? Was it Connor? He was plenty mad when he found out, but I didn't think he'd resort to putting it in the paper." She paused and then continued. "Was it Baxter's wife? Does his wife know?"

I squeaked out my answer. "Not yet. It was me."

Sasha's jaw dropped. "Why would you do that? What harm was a few little lunch dates doing? Two people finding some joy in the middle of the day? What would possess you to tell the newspaper about it?"

"Listen, I know this won't give you any comfort, but it just happened. I was writing this silly article on Baxter about grilling, and one day I noticed his car at the hotel. There was another car parked next to his. At first, I had no idea it was yours. The next day as I was driving back from getting pie, I saw the two cars side by side again. When I turned in my article to Rocky, it just kind of slipped out."

"Slipped out? Are you going to ruin my life because it just slipped out? If this gets out...well, you don't really know Baxter. He's going to be boiling mad. I wouldn't want to be Rocky Whitson if he goes after him."

"I know. What happened is my fault, and that's kind of why I'm here right now. So, there's that and one other little item."

"What, now are you going to tell me he has a sexually transmitted disease or something?"

"No. I mean, I don't know."

"Then what?"

"I was wondering what you could tell me about your ex-husband." She slammed her hand down on the table.

"Really? You want to know about him? Are you tracking my love life? Are you some kind of twisted pregnant stalker? You're sick, you know that?"

I began to think she was right, but twisted or not, I went on.

"Do you think he could be behind all the animal thefts in town?" I asked.

"What the hell?...." She stopped mid-sentence, before launching a new string of insults. I could tell she was picturing her ex and his love for animals.

I asked again. "What do you think?"

She stood up, throwing the towel on the table. "I think you need to get out of here. I'm finished talking to you. March your butt over to that thing you call a newspaper, and tell Rocky Whitson if he publishes any part of this story, I'll sue. Let alone what Baxter will do to him. Got that?"

"Got it." I grabbed my bag and left Benny's as quickly as I could. Once in the car I phoned Rocky.

"So she's going to sue me. How?" he said, after I relayed the information.

"You can't blame her. You're ruining her name and her reputation in this town."

"She ruined her reputation all by herself. I wasn't the one who was checking into the hot sheets motel every day with the local superstar real estate agent. I don't think she was checking out his new listings."

"She kept talking about how violent Baxter could become if he found out about our little spying adventure. I think she's really kind of scared of the guy."

"True love ain't what it used to be, I suppose. Why were you there so early? You usually load up on calories a little later in the day."

"I needed her old address to visit her ex-husband. I have a theory on the animal thefts."

"Do tell."

"It's probably nothing, but I smelled paint at Birdie's Diner last night. Then I saw a smiley face on the wall."

"You've lost me."

"That's Sasha's ex-husband's trademark. He's a painter. I just thought I would go talk to him on the pretense of wanting a mural on our nursery wall."

"You never know. He could be a dangerous criminal. Give me his address and I'll meet you there."

I debated giving him the address given how quickly he ran with the last bit of information I gave him.

"I'm grabbing my keys right now," he said.

He was right. If this smiley-face painter was the thief, he might not be right in the head. Having someone else along could be safer. I tried not to think about the fact that I was bringing the privacy-invading Rocky along as my bodyguard. I gave him the address, and we met at the curb just a few minutes later.

The house at one time had been a springtime blue, but now paint was peeling around the shutters and had faded to a dingy gray. For a guy who was a painter he didn't take very good care of his own property. Sasha had said it was a rental, but what landlord would keep a house in this condition? Living in a depressing place like this would make any wife leave. The front door hung slightly askew from the hinges. We tapped on the dirt-smudged glass.

"Yoo hoo? Anybody home?" I said in my most nonthreatening voice.

"Who says 'yoo hoo'?" Rocky said, eying me sideways.

"Friendly people?"

"Oh right. We're being friendly. Uh...Yoo hoo..." He turned to me. "Sounds stupid."

"What do you want to say? 'It's the media. Give us a statement?'"

He grinned. "I kind of like that."

I knocked again, causing the cheap tin on the door to rattle. Still no answer.

"Doesn't look like anybody's home." We heard the sound of a door closing, coming from the back of the house.

"Maybe he's coming in from the yard. He could have been rinsing out brushes or something."

We waited for a few minutes more, listening for footsteps nearing the front door. Rocky knocked on the door again. If someone was in the backyard or even somewhere in the house, they had to hear us now.

"Could it be what we heard was someone going into the backyard instead of inside the house?" I asked.

"Worth a try."

We stepped off the front porch and went around to the backyard. Rocky looked over the six foot pine privacy fence as a car sped by on the street behind us.

"Hot damn."

"What?"

Ignoring all rules about breaking and entering, Rocky opened the gate.

"Aren't we committing some sort of a crime here?" I said.

"Not when someone is in possession of stolen items," Rocky said.

Lined up as if on display at a museum were the three stolen animals. The summer sun beat down on the cow from Cattleman's Call. He looked a little worse for wear with the move. Lonnie Carello would not be happy to see that Holman made a small hole and a scratch in the side of the cow. The soup-can chicken from Birdie's Diner had a stray can dangling near a wing. Luckily Charlie Loper's prize horse came through without any damage. If you squinted your eyes a bit, they almost looked real. Rocky pulled his camera out of his bag, and began snapping pictures at a furious pace.

"This is rip-snortin' wonderful. You and your smiley face theory have led us to the thief, or at least the stolen items. Maybe I can print these in color. I'll use the headline 'Crazy Smiley Face Painter Hoards Herds.' It's like poetry. If I hurry, I can get it in the online version of the paper within the hour."

He stuffed his camera back in his bag and headed out the fence gate.

"Where are you going?" I asked.

"This is big news. You have your car. You'll be fine."

He left me standing there alone in the backyard. What would possess a person to want to steal these tacky things, I thought. I pulled out my cell phone and dialed the Pecan Bayou Police Department.

"Pecan Bayou Police, " Mrs. Thatcher answered.

"Hi. It's Betsy. I think I've found the missing animals. " Mrs. Thatcher announced my news to anyone within hearing distance. A whoop went up behind her.

"Hold on, dear. I'll get your father on the phone. He's in a meeting, but he'll want me to buzz in for this. Oh, and be sure to get off your feet. That baby needs his rest after all this. "

Within the minute my father came on the line.

"That's great, Betsy. Unfortunately I'm in the middle of a hurricane planning meeting right now. I'll get over there just a little bit later with the truck to pick up the evidence."

"Okay." It didn't look like the animals were going anywhere.

"Do you see Mr. Holman anywhere?" my dad asked.

"Rocky and I knocked on the door several times but there was no answer. He's not here. Maybe he's out casing the giant weinerschnitzel in front of Helmuts B & B."

"Good. We'll have to put out an APB on him. Now get out of there and get home." He was right. I was starting to feel very unsafe. I couldn't be sure, but the soup-can chicken seemed to be glaring at me. I backed out of the yard, closing the gate securely behind me.

CHAPTER 17

When I made it back home, the excitement of talking to Sasha and then finding the stolen animals started to take its toll on me. Back in my non-pregnant days I probably would have fired up the computer and cranked out a column. Not today. I had my feet up on the couch when Leo called.

"Hi Bets. We just took a break so I'm calling to check in on you. Are you getting some rest today?"

"Yeah, I've rested a bit." That was sort of true.

"Any word from the boys today?" Leo asked.

"No, not today," I replied. Then I couldn't help myself. "I think we found the thief," I blurted out.

"We? Who is 'we'? Betsy, please tell me you haven't been out chasing down leads on this silly animal theft. My work schedule is stressful enough with this hurricane and knowing I can't be at home with you. I need to know that you're home safe and sound, not out putting yourself and our baby at risk."

"But Leo..."

"No. What you are doing is dangerous, and you have to think of the baby." Now he was being silly. Dr. Randall had told me I was having a very healthy pregnancy. Leo was acting like I had been confined to bed rest until the baby came. I loved that he was very protective of me, but sometimes it was just too much.

"Look, Leo. You know I've been driving to Benny's every day to get my piece of pie. This all just sort of happened along the way."

"Along the way? You're a drive-by detective now?"

"Yes. It's amazing, if you ask me."

"I didn't ask, and I can also tell when you're stretching the facts, Bets."

"Okay," I admitted. "I've probably done a little more than what I've been telling you, but Leo, I'm so bored here at home waiting for the baby and not having the boys around. You can understand that, can't you?"

He sighed. "I know you'd rather be doing more, but it's just for a little while longer. So how on earth did you catch the animal thief?"

"I figured it out right after we staked out Birdie's Diner..."

"What? When did you do that?"

"Uh ... did I forget to mention that part? It's not important."

"Betsy!"

"It's a long story, but I figured out that the thief was a local wannabe painter and we found all three of the stolen items in his backyard."

"You and Aunt Maggie?"

"No. Rocky and I. Maggie and Danny were with me on the stakeout, which really wasn't so good because we were asleep in the car when the thief stole the soup-can chicken. It should be in the paper tomorrow."

"Do the police know?"

"Dad is in a meeting, but as soon as it's over, he's going to go pick up the animals."

"What about the painter? When is he going to arrest him?"

"As soon as they find him. He wasn't home when we found the statues." I yawned.

"You sound tired. How are you feeling?"

"Good. I appreciate you calling, as you can see I've been a little preoccupied. I'm feeling fine. I know you like constant updates about the baby. When something happens, I'll let you know."

I heard a phone ring in the background. "At least let somebody know. I have to go now, but promise me you'll take it easy. You've cracked the police department's only case. Take this lull in crime-solving as a sign. No more staking out restaurants and finding stolen property. Will you promise me?"

"I promise."

After hanging up, I knew Aunt Maggie would want to know about what was in Connor Holman's backyard.

"I'll be darned," she said a few minutes later. "That's beyond weird."

"Oh." I jumped.

"Betsy? Is something wrong?" she asked.

"Maybe." The baby had just given me an NFL-worthy kick, but then settled down again. "No, nothing's wrong. I'm fine." I felt a sudden tightening around the baby.

"Betsy? Are you still there?"

I answered with an exhale. "Sure. I'm doing better now. The baby's movement feels different somehow. I can't explain it."

"That sounds like labor to me."

"No. I've had a baby before. This is not labor. It's just being nine months pregnant and stretched every which way."

"Okay. You should know. It's been a long time since I was expecting."

"Thanks, I appreciate you trusting me on this."

"I still think it might be a good idea to check in with the doctor."

"You worry too much."

We hung up the phone, and before I could put it away, it rang again.

"Really, I'm not having a baby!" I answered.

A man's voice spoke on the other end. "You won't be if you don't keep your nose out of everyone's business. You've been warned. Go have your baby and leave this alone, or both you and your baby will die." A click sounded on the other end.

I released a breath I didn't even know I was holding. There had been so much hate in that voice. My hand shook as I set down the phone. How did anyone even know I figured out where the animals were? I pulled up the online version of the Pecan Bayou Gazette on a hunch. My suspicion was confirmed. Rocky had posted pictures of the animals in Connor Holman's backyard. Under Rocky's headline was a second lead-in: *Happy Hinter Finds Stolen Menagerie.*

Rocky had even put the photo of the animals above the picture of Hurricane Ezra, the news story the rest of the state would have led with. According to Rocky this was the real news in Pecan Bayou. Millions of people were heading north to evacuate a killer hurricane, but more importantly three fake animals were stolen and caged up cruelly behind a privacy fence.

I clicked off the computer and decided maybe it was time to finish packing my bag for the hospital. I searched for my extra phone charger to put in, and then carried it to the front door. If this baby was coming, the least I could do was to prepare for it. I couldn't believe in just a short time this little person who had been happily inside me for the last nine months would be here to hold in my arms. I felt myself tearing up. Another joy of pregnancy and increased hormonal levels was crying at the drop of a hat. I couldn't even trust myself to watch the Hallmark Channel without a big box of Kleenex next to me on the couch.

As I set the bag down, I felt a sense of melancholy. I could call Aunt Maggie, but I knew I needed more than a phone call. I grabbed my keys and the bag and headed for her house. If I was starting labor, at least I would be with someone. Leo had begged me to stay home, but this was my second home. When I told him about the crank call I had just received, I knew he would approve.

Aunt Maggie greeted me with open arms, of course.

"I'm so glad you came over Betsy. You know how I worry with you being alone over at your house so much." Maggie fussed over me as I settled in on the living room couch, hugging a pillow.

"No need. I'm fine." She surveyed my expression.

"You don't look so good. Are you sure..."

"I'm sure. No labor."

"You know until the hurricane passes and Leo's back by your side all the time, would you consider just staying here with me for a while? It would really make me feel a whole lot better."

"You're probably right. If it's not an imposition, I think that's a good idea. I'd love to stay here with you.."

"Oh Danny will be so excited."

"Is he at day-habilitation today?"

"Yes. They're still open. You know they'll close as soon as the weather sets in. He gets stir crazy when he's home too much. Let him have some time with his friends."

"Do you want me to go with you to get him this afternoon?"

"No, you stay here and rest. He'll be so excited to see you here when he gets home. If you stay here tonight, what about Butch?"

I had completely forgotten about our weimaraner. "Oh no..." I started to get up to get my keys.

"No, no. You just sit there, baby girl. I'll run over and pick him up and drop him by Dr. Springer's office. It might be a good idea just to board him there until after the storm anyway."

"Thanks," I said.

"No problem. You just relax and try not to worry."

Once again I felt that intense tightening on my belly. I reached down and caressed it. This time it was even more intense than the last time. Aunt Maggie came over and put her arm around me.

"Is that a labor pain?"

"No. I don't think so. It's just so strong. Still though, I don't have any pain."

"I think you're having Braxton Hicks. Do you remember those from Zach?"

She was right. I did have the same experience with Zach. The tightening was often mistaken for labor. It felt like labor without the pain. Many women rush to the emergency room with Braxton Hicks to find out they were nowhere near delivering the baby.

Relief rushed over me as the painless contraction ceased. "Oh, Aunt Maggie. I'm so glad I'm here. It just helps to talk to you."

"Well we can at least hope that's what you're feeling. So can you tell me if it's a boy or a girl?"

"No. You're just going to have to wait like everybody else."

"I'm just dying to know. There's a betting pool down at The Best Little Hairhouse in Texas."

"There too?"

"Just because the ladies don't hang out at Bubba's Beer and Bait doesn't mean we can't have a little wager now and again."

"And what did you bet?"

"You have a few secrets, so I guess that's the secret I'll keep from you." She smiled at her sense of power. Once more I felt the tears coming on. Could she understand how safe and secure I felt here in her home? So many things had been going on, I didn't realize how much I needed her company.

Maggie reached up and brushed a tear off my cheek. "Oh, all right. I'll tell. I think it's going to be a girl."

*****

An hour later Maggie returned with Danny who was indeed overjoyed I was spending the night. My father stopped by Aunt Maggie's for a sandwich after the hurricane meeting.

"Have you seen the Gazette online?" I asked.

"As a matter of fact I have. Someone at the meeting asked me if I should let all of my deputies go home and just put you on the payroll. You might get a cold shoulder around the department. It looks pretty bad when our trained detectives get shown up by the Happy Hinter."

"She's just like Batman. She gets the bad guys," Danny said, squirting ketchup on his ham sandwich.

"You were right about my heightened sense of smell. First, I smelled paint, and then I found the smiley face. Once I found it, I knew who had taken the soup-can chicken."

"Yeah, well next time let me in on it."

"Ah come on, Judd. Let your daughter have her moment in the sun," Maggie said.

I debated whether I should tell my dad about the threatening phone call. He was already handling a lot between the storm and thefts. I could hold onto that information for a little while longer. His mood would improve once he had Connor Holman behind bars. I would tell him after he'd locked Holman up. He was just a crazy animal hoarder. Not exactly a murderer.

"So are you going to arrest Holman tonight?" I asked. He reached over and grabbed some onions and added them to his second sandwich.

"Yes ma'am. As soon as I finish up here. I guess I don't need to tell you how pleased I am you've decided to stay with Maggie and Danny."

"You don't."

"With everyone so busy with the hurricane, I'm just lucky we can take care of this guy before we have to shelter the town."

"I'm going to love hearing what led him to it."

"Stuff like this never has a good explanation. You just can't track crazy sometimes."

"I'd like to go with you when you arrest him" I said, taking a bite of my sandwich. I suddenly felt three pairs of eyeballs turned to me.

"Why would you want to do that?" my father asked.

"I sort of feel like this collar is mine. I was the one who solved this case for you, and I should at least be in on the arrest."

"Can I go too, Uncle Judd?" Danny added.

"Judd, you can't let her do this, and Danny you can't go either," Maggie said.

"I have a legitimate reason for being there," I said. "There's something I haven't told you. Before I came over here, a man called and threatened me over the phone."

"Who threatened you?"

"I don't know. Maybe if I heard Holman speak, I could identify his voice. After that, I promise I will sit right here and practice my Lamaze breathing all night." Judd took a moment to think about it.

"What would Leo think of you going along on an arrest at this point in your pregnancy?"

"Oh. He'll be fine. I'll be with you, so he knows I'll be safe. I wouldn't worry about Leo. He trusts me."

CHAPTER 18

A few hours later, we stood on the doorstep of Connor Holman's house. It looked exactly the same as it had earlier, except now clouds moving in were obstructing the sun. The little gray house seemed even more depressing than it had before.

"Okay now Betsy, here's the deal. I'll do all the talking, and you do all the listening. If you think this is the man who threatened you, then you just give me a thumbs-up and head back for the cruiser. Do you understand?"

"Listen, thumbs-up, and back to the cruiser. Got it."

My father pounded on the door.

"Police. We need to talk to you."

Not surprisingly, there wasn't a response to my father's demands. He beat on the door again. No sound from the other side. He opened the screen door and with his finger, gently nudged the wooden inner door. It was not locked. It wasn't even fully shut.

"Are you sure we can do this? Don't you need a search warrant or something?"

"Maybe you'd better get back to the car."

"Not on your life. You think I'm leaving you alone?"

"Darlin', I think you need to go to the car now." I pushed past my father and walked into the house. The smell of rotting flesh hit me. I held my hand up to my mouth, covering my nose.

"Hello? Anybody home?" I called out.

"It's the police Mr. Holman. We need to speak to you about the stolen items in your yard."

I headed toward the living room. "Is anybody here?"

As I walked around the corner of the couch I could see a hand sticking out, splattered with yellow paint. The skin tone was a deep purple with touches of gray. There was no doubt. This person had been dead for a quite some time.

"I think I found something," I said from behind my hand. Holman was sprawled out on the floor. He was as dead as the menagerie that graced his backyard. From the amount of blood and the slash under his chin it looked as if his throat had been cut.

My dad stepped in front of me, now holding a red bandana over his mouth. Seeing the paint- splattered hand, he paced back and began turning me around.

"Enough already. I need to get you back to the car."

This time I didn't argue. It was like the smell of the stinking corpse had taken all of the air out of the room.

"Do you think one of the people he stole from did this?" I said as I crossed the living room back to the front door.

"Maybe. Not sure. Hey, find something to prop that door open, will you?"

I searched around the room and finally picked up a hand-carved horse and stuck it in the doorway. My dad walked over and took in some of the fresh air from the outside. We both took the opportunity to sit on the front step and try to clear the smell of rotting flesh from our noses. I turned to face my dad. "There's something I probably should tell you about Mr. Holman."

"And what would that be?"

"Connor Holman was involved in a love triangle."

"And who would be in this triangle?"

"His ex-wife Sasha Holman was having an affair."

"How do you know this?"

"I happened on the information by accident," I said.

"Did she say he was the kind of fellow who would threaten her or abuse her?"

"I don't think he was too happy about it. She did mention he had a temper. The man she's having an affair with is married. Holman was pretty hard up for money and could have been threatening to expose her."

"And how is it you're having these conversations with this woman?" my dad asked.

"She's Benny's new waitress."

My father smiled. "Ah, the secret life of pie. It's hard for me to believe a guy who got his jollies painting smiley faces everywhere would work a blackmail scheme."

"Still though, we have to consider Holman was the mastermind behind the animal thefts."

"Mastermind? That's a little strong, don't you think? This guy was her ex-husband, correct? Even if he did try to blackmail her lover, it doesn't mean they would even care, and who cares if a divorced waitress is having an affair? She can sleep around all she likes. She doesn't have a position where people question her morals like the president of a church congregation."

"No, but the person she's having the affair with...." I continued.

"You're telling me she was having an affair with Drummond Struthers?"

"No. Baxter Digby."

My father's eyebrows went up. "I'll be doggoned. Is that right? Digby is as slimy as they come around here. You know Mrs. Thatcher bought a house he had listed and had to correct his math at the closing. Seems he made a few errors that accidentally increased his commission."

"It doesn't surprise me," I said. "I also heard he has a reputation for being controlling. Even if he's cheating on his wife, any woman he loves would need to live up to his expectations."

My father scratched his head as he thought about everything, putting together the facts. He pulled out his notebook.

"So the first person I need to talk to is Mr. Baxter Digby, a pretty good suspect at this point in the investigation."

The air in the house felt thick and putrid, and I was starting to feel nauseous.

"You know Dad, don't worry about me waiting in the car. I think I'll call Aunt Maggie to come pick me up. I've had enough of crime-solving for the day."

He reached over with the back of his hand and felt my cheeks. "I think that's a right fine idea, darlin'. I'll take it from here, junior detective." I was never so happy to breathe the fresh, albeit overheated, Texas air as my father walked back into the home of Connor Holman.

I decided before going to the car, I would take a quick walk into the backyard to check on the herd of artificial animals whose eyes had all silently watched the murder of their kidnapper. Would the owners put the animals back up before the storm? I just hoped Charlie Loper's glove would remain secure until his fingers could be repaired and the horse's reigns could be reattached, so he would not go flipping off the rest of Texas.

The rain started to sprinkle on the waiting herd. Not wanting to get soaked, I went out the gate and slid into the car. After calling Aunt Maggie, I started the motor and pushed the air conditioning knob up to high. As I glanced up at the house I began to feel so sorry for Connor Holman. He was killed in his own home. His ex-wife never had a kind word for him, and had already moved on to another man.

Like so many people, Holman wanted his little place in the country. Maybe it was a place reflective of his own childhood, or maybe it was a place from his dreams. His paintings inside showed so many scenes of simple country life. If I had known about his work, I might have bought something. It was such a shame his talent and creativity were now bleeding out in a dark red puddle.

Where was Connor's family? Sasha never mentioned anything about parents being in town. I was so lucky to have family members both older and younger than myself to lean on. Family always chases away the bumps in the night, the forks in the road and the demons of loneliness. Connor was all by himself. I was too late for him in life, but I could help him out in death.

I had spent the better part of this week trying to catch our local thief and now wanted to help him. Maybe I was getting drunk on the mommy Kool-Aid the hormones in my body were producing. Connor was not my child, but he was somebody's. Somebody held him and loved him the way I longed to hold my own child.

I extended the passenger seat back and rested as I waited for Aunt Maggie. It was amazing just last week the sky above was blue and warm. I thought about all those years ago when hurricanes would blow in off the Gulf of Mexico with no warning. Those were before the days of Doppler radar and hurricane hunters. I relaxed in the seat and found myself drifting.

"Hello Miss Happy Hinter." I was standing in the old Pecan Bayou Gazette building, before the fire destroyed it. Standing in front of me was Eula Jean Smith, the victim of the Gazette fire.

"Hi Eula Jean," I answered.

"I wanted to thank you. You solved my murder when people barely knew I was missing. That's what happens when you're an old lady. You get forgotten."

"That's not true. Ruby asked about you."

"Yes. Ruby is good one. Still, though, I had a way of getting left out. I loved filing for Rocky. Such a handsome man. Can't believe he's still single."

"Don't you mean single again?"

"Yes. I suppose you're right."

"I made trouble, you know. That's what lead to my death. Don't make the same mistake."

"Is that your message?"

"What makes you think that?"

"Because each person in my dream is dead and has and brings some cryptic message for me."

Eula Jean walked to the filing cabinet and pulled out a drawer. "Eula Jean? What is your message?" Eula Jean began humming a creepy little tune as she sorted files.

"I think that's where you will get into trouble."

"What trouble?"

"Being left behind."

"Okay, I'll come over there." I started walking towards Eula Jean.

"You need to learn to stay with the action. That's why it took you so long to figure out it was me in the fire. You miss the most important details. You're running out of second chances."

"Betsy?" Maggie was now sitting in the car next to me. "You must've fallen asleep. I knew this was a bad idea. Come on now, I'll take you back home. It's just awful what happened in there. You've pushed yourself too far. Let's just keep take care of you and baby and get you into bed."

As I opened the passenger door of Maggie's ancient station wagon, the car radio was blaring in the background.

Residents of coastal areas should plan to hunker down or evacuate before the storm hits. Residents of central Texas should also have storm supplies at the ready. Once the storm hits land, it can turn into some nasty thunderstorms and tornadoes headed for our region. For that reason Mayor Obermeyer strongly suggests residents move to the storm shelter in Nolan Ryan Middle School. Evacuees from the Houston area and other Gulf Coast communities will be directed to the high school gym. Please make your plans now, and be prepared for this weather system.

"Here they come. The people from the big bad city," Maggie said.

"I like city people," Danny said.

"Yeah, well wait until they find out we only have one movie theater that only shows one movie at a time," Aunt Maggie joked, her eyes never leaving the road.

"I like city people," Danny said. "My doctor is in the city."

"I like city people, too." I agreed with Danny. I had married one after all. I turned my cell phone off when we went into Connor Holman's house, but as I pulled it out of my purse, I saw I had missed a call from Leo. I put in his number.

"Sorry. I was a little busy," I explained.

"Is it the baby?",

"No. I went with my dad somewhere."

"Where?"

"Um. That's not important right now. I know you have a lot going on over there."

"Where, Betsy?" When I didn't answer him right away he repeated his question.

"Where?"

"To arrest Connor Holman," I confessed.

"You what? I thought we discussed this. Just tell me the man went peaceably, and there was no danger to our baby. "

"Uh. Yeah. You cold say he was pretty peaceable."

"Thank goodness."

I couldn't believe I had just gotten away with that one.

"And by the way, I decided to stay with Aunt Maggie, at least for tonight."

"Sounds good to me. I'll come by later. You'll have everything you need there and I'll have..."

"Someone to keep an eye on me?"

"That too. The storm is coming, Betsy, and the idea of you being with Maggie and Danny is a great one." The radio in the background began to echo his forecast.

The storm is moving at about 75 miles per hour. It's expected to make landfall on Galveston Island by early Thursday. From there it is predicted to move towards our area. As the storm lessens over land, there is still a chance of heavy thunderstorms, winds and tornadoes.

"Betsy, are you in a car?" Leo continued. "I hear the radio."

"Oh yes. Aunt Maggie and Danny picked me up from Connor Holman's house. My dad didn't want me in there with the crime scene."

"You mean he had those animals in his house?"

He would not be very happy to know I had just found another body. When we got married I sort of promised Leo I would slow down discovering dead people.

"Betsy? Are you still there?" Leo asked.

"Connor Holman was dead when we got there," I blurted out.

"Good grief. Are you telling me you and your dad found him?"

"Yes. But we didn't know he would be dead. You see, I convinced Dad to let me go along to arrest Holman because I got this threatening phone call and we needed to hear his voice so I could identify him."

"That's it. Go home. Do what every other person in Pecan Bayou is doing right now. Get ready for the storm. Oh yeah, and get ready to have our baby. You have plenty to do now, and you certainly don't need to have a ride along with Officer Judd."

He was right. I knew he was right.

"I'll do that. I promise. I'm done. Totally done."

"I'm just glad you're okay. Thank goodness your father was with you this time."

That was it? That was all I was going to get for being nine months pregnant and stumbling onto a crime scene? Something was up.

"So Betsy, you remember me telling you about the guy I met when we flew into the hurricane? The storm chaser?"

The plot thickens. "Yes..." I said warily.

"You're not going to believe this, but he invited me to ride along and chase storms that trigger off of Ezra with him. Isn't that great?"

"And you said no, right? For a minute there I thought you were going to tell me that you planned to be driving around chasing after tornadoes and putting yourself in further danger."

"Well it's not like I'm going to fall out of a plane or anything. Storm chasers almost never get injured. They can see what's coming from miles away."

"And they have the uncontrollable urge to get as close as they can to shoot YouTube videos," I added.

"These guys are pros Betsy. They all have families just like me, and they're not going to put their own lives in danger. These storm chasers have been doing this for years. Actually it's pretty safe." If I could only believe that.

"So, what are you trying to say, Leo?"

"I have this idea that maybe I could just ride along with Nate for a couple of hours during the storm. Not the whole storm, but just a couple of hours. What do you think?"

He did not want to know what I thought. I wanted to be supportive of him. This was Leo's passion, aside from me, of course. How could I stop him from pursuing something as exciting is this? Then there was that little issue of my own jumping into danger catching thieves and stalking cheating real estate agents while pregnant. What's good for the goose...

"Just for a couple of hours?" I asked.

"That's all. I promise."

"Fine. But you had better be here when our baby makes his or her appearance into the world."

"Wouldn't miss it," he said, trying to reassure me.

"I spoke to Zach and Tyler and the camp is preparing for the storm. I also spoke to my mother, and she volunteered to go pick them up."

That was the best news I'd heard all day. I was beginning to like Leo's mother, Gwyn, more and more. I hadn't thought of asking her to pick up the boys at camp. "That is wonderful. Thank your mother for me. Better yet, I think I'll do it myself when I see her in person."

"And Betsy?"

"Yes?"

"You know I love you, don't you?"

"Yes. We're two of a kind, you and me."

CHAPTER 19

"Leo wants to storm chase, " I announced in the car.

"I can't believe you agreed to that," Aunt Maggie said.

"Me either. Say, could you do me a favor before we go home?"

"What do you need?"

"Some chocolate pecan pie."

"In this rain? You know, after all this time, I should have predicted a stop at Benny's."

"I like pie," Danny said.

"Better get two pieces," Aunt Maggie said.

Danny smiled. "Two big pieces."

We pulled into Benny's Barbecue, and I attempted to dash in between rain drops.

"I won't be a minute, " I shouted back to Maggie in the car. I stepped into Benny's where Sasha was wiping down a table and placing dishes into a plastic dish tub. She didn't even attempt to be nice as she glared at me from across the restaurant. Benny put two big pieces of pie into a container and then into a bag.

"Could I speak with Sasha? She's been so... helpful. I just wanted to thank her."

"Sure." He eyed me suspiciously. He had been in the kitchen and within hearing distance earlier.

Sasha narrowed her eyes at me as Benny went into the back, leaving us alone.

"I wish I could say it's nice to see you Betsy, but that would be a lie. My mother told me never to lie."

"Has anyone called you?" I asked.

"No. Did you tell Baxter's wife about us? You're unbelievable, you know that?"

"No. I didn't tell anyone about you." Okay, that was technically wrong. She didn't need to know I talked about her affair with not only Rocky, but my father, Aunt Maggie and Ruby.

"I would never tell his wife," I added.

She slammed the dish tub on the counter. "Then what? I'm kind of busy here. Benny wants every surface scrubbed before we shut down for the storm."

"When was the last time you saw Connor?"

"I don't know. Is he lost or something? Did he wander off in a field of cows somewhere?"

I hesitated a moment. Even if she were divorcing him, there had been love there once. Maybe I should wait for the police to inform her.

"What?" Sasha continued, becoming more irritated. "You have me listening now, but hurry up, will you?"

"No. Maybe I'd better let the police tell you. I shouldn't have said anything. Forget I mentioned it."

"What? Is he okay?" I looked to the floor because I could no longer look her in the eye.

She plopped down into a booth. "You know, of all the people in Pecan Bayou, I probably hate you the most, but if something has happened to Connor, I would rather hear about it from you than from some cop."

I squeezed into the booth across from her and reached out and took one of her hands. First, confusion, then fear registered on her face.

"He was murdered."

She pulled away from me, the back of her head bumping up against the booth.

"Murdered? You must be wrong. Not Connor. Who would murder Connor? Are you sure?"

"Yes. I'm sure."

"What happened?"

"We don't know yet. The police are over there now. It looks like somebody attacked him." She reached for a paper napkin to catch tears that were now forming.

I went on. "You said Digby had a temper. Do you think he could've done something like this?"

Her mascara began to run down her face as her eyes widened at my implication.

"What is it with you? Why are you always trying to tear down Baxter? He would never do anything like this. How dare you. It's bad enough you just told me somebody killed my husband, uh...ex-husband, but then you have to go and say my " She searched for a suitable name for her entanglement with Digby, "... boyfriend... might be the murderer?"

"I'm sorry, but you have to admit that he has a motive. If I came to this conclusion, the police are going to come to it, too. You may as well prepare yourself for it."

"You've got a lot of nerve."

"So you've been here at work all afternoon?" I asked.

"Most of it. We were pretty busy... Oh my God. You're seeing if I have an alibi. You need to leave now. I don't want to talk to you anymore. If you need pie, go buy some of that frozen stuff down at the supermarket."

As I climbed back into Maggie's station wagon, I began to feel the familiar tightening of a Braxton Hicks contraction. I took a deep breath as the painless contraction worked its way through me.

Maggie put her hand on my shoulder and leaned towards me. "Is that labor?"

"Are you going to have the baby?" Danny asked.

"No, Danny, it's just the Braxton Hicks contractions again."

"Tell Mr. Braxton you can't have contractions for him. You're having contractions for us."

"I'll be sure to tell him." I smiled.

"That's it," Maggie said. "Let's get you home before we have anything else happen. I have to get the hurricane supplies ready, and we need to pack a bag if we end up at the shelter."

A feeling of dread came over me. The idea of having a baby in a storm shelter was terrifying.

"Maybe I should just check into the hospital."

"Are you having the baby?" Danny asked again.

"No. I'm not having the baby," I snapped. Danny bit his lip and started blinking rapidly.

"I'm sorry. I was just thinking the hospital might be the best place in case I go into labor."

"I'm all for that," Maggie said. "Why don't you call your doctor?"

I pulled out my phone and dialed my obstetrician, Dr. Randall.

Her receptionist answered the phone. "Betsy, I hate to tell you this, but Dr. Randall had to go down to Houston to help evacuate her elderly mother. We don't expect her back for several days. I guess it's quite an operation to move her out of her assisted living center."

"So you're saying that if I start having contractions in the next twenty-four hours, my obstetrician will not be here?"

"But we hardly could've predicted any of this. We are trying to track down another doctor or possibly a midwife who can pitch in if something happens. It's not the end of the world. Living in a small town you should know doctors can be over-scheduled. Besides, you're the Happy Hinter. You must have some sort of tips on hand for delivering babies?" She laughed, trying to lighten the moment.

These were not the words of reassurance a woman about to deliver wanted to hear. The idea of having this baby with anybody else was frightening.

"So maybe checking myself into the hospital is not a solution?" I said.

"It probably is a good idea. They have backup generators if you should go into labor."

"Do they have midwives at the hospital?"

"They just might!" she exclaimed, as if it were the first time she had considered the possibility. I know she was trying to make me feel better, but the fact she couldn't commit to having a midwife at the hospital was unnerving.

"Great. I'll think about checking myself in."

"Couldn't hurt!" Her voice was way too chipper. She wasn't the one who was facing childbirth in the worst of all possible circumstances. What if there was some sort of complication with the baby? Or me? It was a scary thought.

"Darn it," Aunt Maggie said as I hung up the phone.

"What?"

"We need bottled water."

"Can't we just get some at the shelter?"

"We could, but there's still a possibility we'll be at home without power and water."

I yawned. "Okay. Let's run by the grocery store and pick some up."

"Thanks. I know you're tired and I promise we'll go home right after we pick up a case."

When we entered the store, it looked like a department store toy department the day after Christmas. Shelves were bare, and the few remaining cases of bottled water were now pushed to the front.

Jeff Ellis, Birdie's new boyfriend, put a case into his basket and was about to pick up the last one when Aunt Maggie stepped up.

"Do you need both? We forgot to pick up water."

"Actually, I do. Birdie might need it at the diner," he said, and then his glance fell on me.

"Aren't you the cop's daughter?"

"Yes. I was there the other night when the soup-can chicken was stolen."

"Right. At least they found it. It was my way of expressing my love to Birdie. Junk art gets laughed at, but it is the purest and most ecologically friendly form of art. I can't believe it was ripped right off Birdie's roof. I guess in a way it's a form of flattery. Of course, if the thief stole my chicken *first*, now that would be flattery. Driving through town, you see a giant chicken on the roof of the diner and all of a sudden you find your mouth watering for chicken, am I right? The Cattleman's Call guy actually called Birdie to tell her I had copied him with my chicken on the roof. Did he have a cow on his roof? I don't think so. His cow was out in front. I had no idea the food business in this town was so cutthroat. I tell you it's absolutely cutthroat."

I thought it was pretty interesting he would use the phrase "cutthroat." I wasn't sure if the cause of Connor Holman's death had been released anywhere yet.

"Did you know Connor Holman, the thief?" I said.

"Yes. I've met the guy. There aren't that many other artists in this town. We had a few conversations. He acted like making something out of old cans was pedestrian. You know, a can is a can, but when you throw in raw talent, it turns into a giant chicken. He must have changed his mind about what he considered artistic if he liked it enough to steal it. Shoot, I would have made him one if he had just asked me. I tried calling him this afternoon, but he didn't even answer his phone."

Over in the corner of the grocery I spied Mayor Obermeyer and his wife wheeling a cart full of bottled water. Maybe they could spare one. Before I could get there, my phone rang. I held up a finger to signal one minute to them and swiped the screen. It was my dad.

"Well, Betsy are you having a baby? Because you and Maggie don't seem to be at her house."

"No. We had to stop by the store to get bottled water. But there's nothing left on the shelves here."

"Should've known that. Just wanted to let you know I tried to talk to Baxter Digby. According to his secretary, he's out of the office right now. Maybe I should check the ever-popular Super Stay Motel. Secretary says at the time of Connor Holman's murder, Digby was addressing the League of Women Voters along with Mayor Obermeyer. They were having a "Meet the Candidate" afternoon. Both Baxter and Drummond Struthers were there. There isn't anything more solid than when the mayor provides an alibi. He's a pretty good character witness."

I glanced across the store. Mayor Obermeyer and his wife were standing in line at the register.

"We'd better get going. I'll let you know if I have any baby news." I hung up the phone and headed over to the mayor's line.

"Betsy, there's a shorter line over there," Aunt Maggie said.

"Wait just a minute. Maybe the mayor will share some of the water he has." I pushed past someone and ran into a magazine rack, hurting my side. I held it and gasped.

"Oh my, Betsy, are you having your baby?" Mayor Obermeyer, who had been holding what looked like an old piece of wood, handed it to his wife and took hold of my elbow. I dropped my hand before they could get me to the floor and start telling me to breathe.

"No. I'm not, but thanks for your help. I was wondering if we could have a case of your water?"

"Oh, sure. We'll be glad to share. We're all in this together, after all," he said, looking around making sure his constituents heard him.

"Why are you carrying an old log around?" I asked, looking at the gnarled log now resting in his wife's arms like a baby.

"That, my dear, is the most precious artifact of Pecan Bayou. It was one of the first pecan trees planted here by my ancestor Tobias Obermeyer. It is the very reason this town prospered. Well, that and the railroad. As long as we're in storm mode, it is my sovereign duty to protect this precious piece of history." It looked like a wormy piece of wood to me, but I nodded in mock appreciation.

"I also wanted to ask you a question about the meeting you had with the League of Women Voters."

"Yes. It was quite a full afternoon. We had both of the candidates who are running for city council. I really feel like the ladies got a good feel for the men and their platforms. Are you thinking about joining the League of Women Voters? We always need our soldiers in the trenches."

"True, and what a wonderful job the ladies do, but I was just wanting to ask you about Baxter Digby. How long was his speech to the women?"

"Each of the candidates spoke for ten to fifteen minutes. Why do you ask?"

"After he finished speaking, did he stay to hear the other speech? Did the candidates debate?"

"That would've been really wonderful, but no, Mr. Digby had to go. He had a showing on the other side of town. There were some new folks visiting us. We have to do everything we can, to encourage people to move to our area. Still though, he gave the ladies a humdinger of a speech."

"Yes," I said. "He certainly has a way with the ladies."

Obermeyer smiled and nodded, and then stopped abruptly, catching my meaning.

Then his grin widened, as he homed in on another tool of persuasion Digby possessed. Politicians. Always figuring the angle.

CHAPTER 20

The rain was starting to pick up as we made our way home. The skies had turned a shadowy gray, and I felt myself drifting with the sound of Aunt Maggie's windshield wipers methodically going back and forth.

As we pulled into her driveway, Rocky emerged from his pickup parked on the street.

"What are you doing here?" I said as I grabbed a bag out of the back of the car. Danny lifted the case of water, and we all ran for the door as the rain came down in earnest. Rocky took my bag as Aunt Maggie opened the door.

"I think I'm the one with the questions," he said as he followed Aunt Maggie to the kitchen, putting the bag on her counter.

"For me? You saw everything I saw in Connor Holman's backyard."

"Here I have one of my reporters witness a crime scene, and you can't even pick up the phone?"

"It only just happened, Rocky, and I'm a columnist, not a reporter. Besides, just because I saw it doesn't mean I want you to print it in the newspaper."

"Like I always say Betsy, news is news." He pulled out a mini voice recorder and pointed it at me. "Now, can you describe the scene, using as many adverbs and adjectives as you possibly can."

Another Braxton Hicks tightened over my abdomen. I put my hand on my belly as if to still it.

Rocky's eyebrows lifted in surprise. "Oh boy. Maybe you should sit down. I keep forgetting you're in a delicate condition."

"No. I'm fine," I said, raising a hand to push him away.

"Great! Describe the crime scene."

"No," I said simply.

"What do you mean no? You can't say no. You work for me and you were a witness, so you need to tell me what you saw."

"Okay, Pecan Bayou's only horse thief is dead. There was a lot of blood. It is now under investigation by the Pecan Bayou Police Department."

"That's it?"

"That's it."

"You're killing me, kid."

"Sorry. I also should tell you I warned Sasha Holman you were planning to publish a story about the affair. She's not too happy with me."

"Not happy with you? Shouldn't she be unhappy with me? I'm not going to put any names in the paper. I'm going to word it like 'What city council candidate was recently spotted at the Super Stay Motel with a local waitress?' That's not too bad."

"That's awful Rocky. What if Drummond Struther's family thinks it's him? He's a nice guy, for goodness sakes. He didn't do anything. You can't write that. In one sentence you've not only destroyed one man's life, but two. You can't run it. Not everything is news, and this stuff is destructive. I thought you were a pacifist. Besides, I'm starting to hear Digby has a temper. You may be throwing a rock at a hornet's nest with this story."

Rocky blew out a sigh. "Maybe. Tell you what. I'll make you a deal. I won't run the sleaze about Baxter Digby if you will describe the crime scene to me."

"I'll tell you what. I'll make *you* a deal," I repeated after him, nodding my head to the side. "You don't run the Baxter Digby story, and I won't tell you about the crime scene. You could spend your time reporting stories appropriate for this paper like the Pinewood Derby or the church bazaar. That's the kind of stuff a small-town newspaper normally runs. They do not print stories about what people do at the Super Stay Motel."

"Yeah, well if I did, I bet circulation would skyrocket. If I have a story to tell, baby, I'm going to tell it." Rocky turned and started heading for the door. "If you do decide you want to describe the crime scene to me, you know where to find me."

Maggie came into the room holding a suitcase and set it by the door.

"Rocky are you going to the shelter?" she asked.

"Not until they tell me I have to go. Nicholas and I are going to be getting as much footage as we can. I send him pictures from my cell and within ten minutes they're in the online version of the Gazette. Betsy, if you weren't out of commission, I'd have you out there with your cell phone taking pictures. I'm working in coordination with Stan at NUTV and we're going to cover the storm like never before. This is such an exciting time."

I couldn't get over how much he sounded like Leo.

"Well then, you be careful, you here?" Aunt Maggie said.

"Yes ma'am. I hear." Rocky tipped his hat and stepped back out into the rain.

CHAPTER 21

As we prepared supper I was very happy when Leo's mother knocked at the door. The boys came in and ran to me for a hug. It felt so good to have them back again.

"Where should we put our stuff?" Tyler asked.

"I think it's already in the perfect place there by the door. We may be relocated to the shelter in the next twenty-four to forty-eight hours," Maggie said.

Zach looked like he had grown a full inch, and his sunburned face was different somehow. More like a young man and less like the little boy I had always known.

"Wow, Mom," he said his eyes scanning my form. "You look really big."

Leave it to the ones you love to tell you how fat you look.

"Yeah. Just how much bigger will you get?" Tyler said, wrinkling his nose in disgust.

"I think I'm pretty well maxed out."

"That's good, because if you keep gaining weight like this, you'll be ginormous," Tyler said. Ginormous? Was I that big?

"Thanks for making her feel so good about it," Gwyn said. "She's gained weight, but that's because there's another whole person in there. In the last month or so the baby has grown five to eight inches and has probably put on at least four pounds. So it's not your mom who is gaining the weight, it's the baby."

Having a science teacher in the family was proving useful. At least somebody was on my side.

"Sorry," Tyler said.

"Yeah," Zach added. "More of you to love, right?" He looked around the room and then under the table. "Where's Butch?"

"He's at Dr. Springer's office. She's boarding all the dogs and cats until the storm passes."

"Can we get him as soon as it's over?"

"Sure."

That evening as the storm was neared the island of Galveston, my family was in "hunker down" mode in Pecan Bayou. Leo and my dad came in a little bit after the boys, and we sat around the table discussing our options.

"What if you have the baby when the hurricane comes, Mom?" Zac said, after wolfing down his dinner. Were they feeding him at that camp?

"I'm just hoping the baby will wait until the storm has passed."

"Well one thing predictable about babies," Aunt Maggie said, "is they're not predictable."

"We're all hoping that the baby waits until after the storm. That way we'll all have more time to be there," Leo added.

"Especially you, Dad. You need to be here," Tyler said.

"Besides boys," Judd said as he buttered a hot roll, "your mother has been too busy finding bodies again to have a baby."

I shot him a glance. "I don't think that that's a good topic for dinner time."

"You're right," Leo said. "We'll save it for dessert." The boys laughed.

"We already know about it. Grandma Gwyn told us on the way here." Tyler said.

"Seriously, Mom, this guy stole a chicken made out of cans?" Zach asked.

"Dang. I wished I'd seen that," Tyler said.

"I loved that chicken," Danny said.

"Not to worry. It'll be back up and crowing on the roof in no time." My father said.

"How did you figure it out?" Tyler asked.

Leo answered before I could utter a word. "Pregnant nose. Ever since your mother has been pregnant, any smell can set her off. She smelled paint, and let's face it, The Happy Hinter hasn't solved a crime in months. When I married her, I thought she just spent her time telling people how to caulk around the tub."

"You must mean the happy homicide hunter," My father said as his phone rang in his pocket.

"Excuse me for a minute." He rose from the table and went into the next room. The boys began telling us details of the day-to-day life at summer camp.

When my father returned, he had his keys in his hands. "That was Mrs. Thatcher. They're getting all kinds of calls at the station. A tornado touched down outside of Andersonville. The chief wants me down at the shelter early. We're relocating all the emergency services to that location."

Leo's phone beeped in his pocket. He pulled it out and swiped the screen to read a text.

"Okay. Nate is texting he's going to be chasing this one and wonders if I would like to come along."

"Oh, Leo. Now?" said Gwyn.

"How are you feeling Betsy?" he asked.

"I'm feeling okay, I guess."

"Then if it is okay with you, I'll be back before you know it. It's just a couple of hours, I'm sure. I'll have my cell phone" He held it up in front of his face. "Uh...I'll charge my cell in Nate's car, but I'll be there if you need me. Nate assured me that babies take precedence over funnel clouds."

I let out a long exhale. I couldn't say no. I wasn't in labor, and the chances of me having the baby in the next few hours were small. Technically, I wasn't due for at least a week. I had to let him go.

"Okay..."

He jumped up and kissed me. I pushed him away, "But promise me you will be careful? Please? "

"Yes. Of course."

"What about the weather bureau? Don't they need you? " Leo's mother asked.

"I'm actually working for the bureau on the road. I'll be sending back videos and measurements."

Leo pulled his keys out of his pocket, ready to rush out the door.

"Wait! Before everybody takes off, we need to have some sort of a plan," I said, feeling slightly abandoned.

"You're right," Leo's mother said.

"I'm going to be keeping my eye on the storm as it goes inland. If it looks like it's heading towards Pecan Bayou, then I would suggest all of you go to the shelter. It has better walls to sustain hurricane force winds and tornadoes. Everybody needs to stay together."

"That's true," Gwyn said. "Even though I've gotten out of Galveston, I know I can still get hit by the weather, and folks, we're not only on storm watch but baby watch." She smiled knowingly in my direction.

"Well then I guess it's settled," Judd said. Everybody get your bag packed and be ready to relocate to the shelter."

After Judd and Leo left, we cleaned up the dishes and everyone settled down in front of the TV. We might as well be comfortable until the call to cram the entire town into a school gym.

All the local channels were now covering the hurricane nonstop. It always amazed me that the networks would put some weather guy right in front of the storm surge in Galveston. I would never understand the motivation to put someone in danger like that. Then again, it thrilled my own husband to be in league with the storm chasers. There was a time people avoided a storm, not break their necks to document it. Everyone wanted to stare at those cell phone videos and to take pictures that could go on Instagram. We were all addicted to instant news gratification.

"Betsy," Leo's mother asked. "Do you have your bag packed? I mean your baby bag packed in case you go into labor?"

"Yes. I just wish I could pack whatever the hospital uses to lessen the pain of childbirth. That would be nice. My doctor went to Houston, and her receptionist was hoping she'd find someone who could deliver a baby."

"What about the local EMTs?"

I thought about Orley Ortiz, the EMT who always kidded me about finding bodies. Most of the emergency personnel would be answering 911 calls that would inevitably come in with the storm. If it was a quiet night, he would be around, but if it wasn't I was on my own. When I thought of all the crime scenes where we had crossed paths, I never imagined he might deliver my baby.

"Think of it. You might go into the shelter with two children and come out with three," Gwyn said.

That thought was pretty overwhelming. I was starting to suffer from baby overload. I longed for the days when conversation would be about someone else in the room.

Gwyn sighed. "I wish we knew if it was a boy or a girl."

"Mom knows," Zach said.

"Yeah Betsy," Tyler said. "Why don't you tell us if the baby is a boy or girl?"

"I can't. I want it to be a surprise. To tell the truth I'm not totally sure myself. I did see the sonogram, but..."

"Does it feel like a boy?" Danny asked.

"I don't know. I've only ever been pregnant with a boy, but it feels kind of like Zach did." The boys started jumping around.

"It's a boy! We're going to have a brother."

"We'll be the Fitzpatrick boys." They shouted and jumped around the living room.

After celebrating their new brother, the boys grabbed pillows off the couch and settled down in front of the TV.

"Can we all sleep out here tonight in the living room?" Zach asked.

"I don't see why not. If we have to grab our stuff and go to the shelter, it might be a pretty good idea," I said.

"Can we watch a scary movie?" Tyler asked.

"No," Danny said flatly.

"Danny doesn't like scary movies," I said.

"It's not like they're real or anything," Tyler laughed. The look on Danny's face indicated Tyler had made him feel silly.

"Nevertheless, he doesn't like them." We finally decided to watch a series of sitcoms with the weather warnings running along the bottom of the television. The entire family settled in watching the aimless jokes and canned laughter.

Pulling up a blanket around me, I listened to the sound of the rain pelting the windows. Then I smelled it, fresh paint. Had Aunt Maggie been painting recently? Leo's joke about my pregnant nose had never been truer. It was almost overwhelming.

I looked around the room. It was now quiet and I saw Connor Holman standing in the door. He wore a white t-shirt with a smiley face on it. At his throat was a deep gash leaking blood, dripping onto the floor.

"You never knew me."

"Only in death."

"I didn't have many friends in life. Glad I made one in death."

"Who killed you, Connor?"

"For me to know, and you to find out."

"Couldn't make it easy on me, huh? I saw some of your work. You were good. I loved the way you painted animals. You captured their beauty."

"Thank you. Animals are pure and honest. They would never cheat on you. They will always help you step into the wind."

"Why did you steal the animals?"

"They were beautiful. I wanted to paint them all. It started with the horse, and then I just couldn't stop myself. I needed to see those animals all the time. I had to paint them. Does that sound strange to you?" If he only knew.

"Your work was so good, why did you sign it with a smiley face? You had to know it made your paintings look amateur," I said, knowing the truth might hurt his feelings. Then again, he was a ghost.

"You don't know creative expression. It didn't feel right to me signing the name society had given me. Inside I felt like that little happy yellow guy, mostly... except when I found out about Sasha and that salesman."

"So you knew?"

"Sure. Sasha was much more complicated than I was. When she came home from work smiling all the time, I knew it had nothing to do with making biscuits for Benny."

"So what is your message for me?"

"Find my killer and when you do, be safe. The roads will be busy with comings and goings."

"Do you mean the killer or the baby coming?"

"Both."

Danny and the boys laughed at a wisecracking teenager on the television, making me jump. I yawned and stretched, feeling the baby slide to one side. Comings and goings echoed in my brain. Connor Holman had joined the grisly crew delivering warnings. He wanted me to solve his murder as I had for the other victims from my dreams.

I kept thinking there was some item I had missed at the crime scene. There had to be something there that would point to his killer. I thought back on his paintings. He painted all of those beautiful scenes, and then plastered a smiley face in the corner. It was a shame he didn't go with a more professional trademark, because from what I had seen, his work was not that bad. There is a market for scenes of rural life, but like so many creative people, he didn't know how to promote his own work.

Maggie had been snoring quietly beside me. I looked up to see a notice running on the bottom of the TV screen.

"Residents...of...Pecan...Bayou...a...storm...is...imminent...for...your...ow ease...report...to...the...assigned...shelter..."

"Okay everybody we're traveling," Aunt Maggie said. "Let's get going to the shelter. Everybody grab your bags. We're getting in the car in the next five minutes. Danny, get your pillow and your blanket.

"I don't want to go to the shelter," Danny said. He did not do well with abrupt changes in his routine. It was for that reason Aunt Maggie almost never traveled. Spending a night in a hotel could be extremely stressful for both of them.

"It'll be okay Danny. We'll all be there with you," Tyler said. Zach put his arm around his cousin. "Do you want to sit next to me in the car?"

"I want to stay here."

"I know, but we'll have fun, and some of your friends might be there too," Aunt Maggie said.

"Where?"

"At the shelter. Let's go see."

"Okay," Danny said reluctantly.

A few minutes later, as I scooted over onto the seat, I suddenly felt what started out to be a Braxton Hicks contraction. Something about this painless contraction did not seem quite so painless. I shifted in my seat.

"Everything okay, Betsy?" Leo's mother asked.

"Fine. I'm just fine."

CHAPTER 22

Although I was sure I was in the early stages of labor something was bugging me. It was a nagging thought that pulled me away from the storm shelter.

The cryptic messages were finally making sense, and I was pretty sure I knew what the people in my dreams were trying to tell me. If I followed through on their clues, they could point me directly to the murderer.

Still, though, I felt trapped riding along in my aunt's station wagon. If I could just take a half hour and check it, I could concentrate on the baby. I opened my phone and called Leo.

"How is the storm chasing going?"

"Great. We've seen a funnel cloud from less than a mile. It's awesome! Oh no. Are you having the baby?" Leo asked, with just a little disappointment in his voice.

"Doing fine." I wasn't lying. I was doing fine in progressing towards labor. Labor could take anywhere from ten to twenty hours. He would be back in plenty of time.

"Good. You had me worried there for a minute."

"Are you going to be back soon? We're evacuating to the shelter."

"You of all people should know it's pretty hard to predict a storm. I promise we're heading your way. From the way it looks, I should be out with them for less than an hour, and I'll join you at the shelter. As exciting as all of this is, I also have the feeling that this could be the day for the baby."

Me too, I thought. "Well that's good to hear. I really want you with me tonight." I looked around the car to make sure my fellow passengers could not hear Leo's side of the conversation. If I wanted to run a side errand, this was going to be the only way to do it.

"Yes. I guess I could do that," I said into the phone. My words confused Leo on the other end.

"I'm sorry, Bets. What did you say?"

I continued with my fictional conversation. "Okay. I'll tell you what. I'll meet you in front of the police station. That works for me. How about you?"

"The police station? Why would I want you standing outside at the police station in this weather? You should go to the shelter with the family. Are you feeling okay?"

"Okay then, I guess I'll see you in about an hour in front of the police station. Don't be late." I clicked the phone shut and turned and smiled as if nothing was out of the ordinary.

Aunt Maggie's head jerked around from the front seat. "Did you say you're meeting Leo at the police station in an hour? What is he, crazy? Let me talk to him on that phone."

I held up the phone to her.

"Sorry, he already hung up. They were zeroing in on another tornado."

"You have to be nuts if you think I'm going to let you stand out in front police station," Maggie said.

My little subterfuge wasn't working. I scrambled for a better reason to be at the station.

"What he really said was Dad asked him to ask me to go into the police station and pick up some red flares for the storm."

"Well that's simple. We can do that on our way."

This was not getting any easier. "No, Aunt Maggie. I really want you to get the boys to the shelter. This is really no big deal and I'm just glad I can help, what with the police force being so busy with the storm. I think the flares are in the back closet. It won't take me long, but I do have to search a little for them. By the time I find everything, Leo will be there to pick me up."

Leo's mother pursed her lips and began shaking her head. "Why don't I come with you? What if you go into labor?"

"No, Gwyn. I really want you to be there with the boys. Tyler especially needs you there." I pushed hard on her fraternal grandmother instinct.

"Is your cell phone charged?"

I pulled out my phone and checked the bars. "Yes I'm fully charged. See?" I held it up for the entire car to count the bars.

"I'll be fine. You know, some women go two weeks over their due dates. If I feel anything suspicious, I'll call you, and you can rush over to pick me up before Leo gets there. It's only an hour."

"I really don't know about this, Betsy," Maggie said as she pulled up to the police station.

"Call Dad and check if you don't believe me."

Maggie thought for a moment, and then raised her hand to shew me out of the car. "I don't like this, and if I don't hear something from you in the next hour, we're stormin' the station, do you hear?"

I pulled myself out of the car and waved goodbye, then pulled out my key to the station. My father gave it to me years ago when I was still a teenager. He wanted me to be able to get in the building even if they were locked down.

As the door opened, the air in the station felt different. Most of the time there were emergency lights flooding the hallways, but tonight it was very dark inside. The police department building had been shut down to move the base of operations to the shelter. Even cops need to be safe.

I felt on the wall and thankfully found a light switch. I knew the stolen items would be in the back of the building, in the impound yard. It was overcast and extremely dark outside, and I wished I had thought to bring a flashlight.

As my eyes adjusted, I could see the outlines of shapes. I knew they were the animals, but they could have been anything, including a person. I found the outdoor flood lights and flipped them on. The beams of white electric light illuminated the eerie black shapes into the animals I had come to examine.

Stepping out into the yard I walked to the side of the cow. Even with the flood lights on, it was hard to see. Relying on my sense of touch, I ran my hand along the lower side of the cow, feeling for the hole I had seen when it stood in Connor Holman's yard.

As I reached down, I felt the tug of the baby. There was a painful pulling down, and I knew I had to be dilating. I looked at my watch deciding to time what I knew was an early contraction. It wasn't an intense contraction, and with Zach's birth, at this point I was still many hours away from delivery. I leaned up against the fence and took a deep breath as the contraction waned.

I went back to the cow, and putting my hand on the rough edge I tried to turn the cow itself. It was too heavy to move. Trying a new approach, I got down on my knees for a view of the underside of the cow. I reached along the crack again, and as I had suspected, there was a ragged hole that had been patched.

The crack led me to what I was looking for. I punched my fist through the patched area and reached in. Was the smiley-face painter's murder connected to whatever was inside this cow?

My fingers landed on something that felt like a paperback book. When I pulled it out, I knew who had slashed the throat of Connor Holman.

What I pulled from the cow was not a book, but a banded stack of bills, reminding me of cash in a bank vault.

Stuffing the cash back up in the cow's stomach, I backed out of the enclosure, turned off the light and returned to the front of the police station. With the crazy message I gave Leo, I knew he would turn the storm chasers our way. He probably thought I was out of my mind and in labor. He'd be right on at least one count, maybe both.

I locked the front door of the police station and felt another contraction. I looked at my watch. It had only been six minutes since the last contraction. This one picked up a little in intensity. The rain and wind whipped around my ankles. I leaned against the wall waiting for the contraction to pass. Six minutes apart wasn't too bad, and it could go on like this for hours. I could do this, I reassured myself.

Panic slowly crept into my forced calm. I was all alone on the deserted Main Street in Pecan Bayou. Everyone who could possibly help me was now in the shelter protected from the storm. The sound of the wind would block out my screams.

For the last two weeks I couldn't avoid everybody and their neighbor asking me if I was in labor. Right now, I would give anything for one person to ask me that irritating question. Yes! I would tell them. I'm in labor.

"Is anybody listening?" I shouted. "I'm in labor!"

A tear escaped from my cheek to the arm I was leaning on. I was going to have to deliver my baby alone in a storm, and it was all my fault. If I had just listened to Aunt Maggie, I wouldn't be in this mess. I was alone. I should have at least shared my suspicions with my father. Maybe I could call Maggie and have her come pick me up. Before I could punch in her number, I spotted car lights approaching. I breathed a sigh of relief. Leo was here. I knew he would save me. I just knew it.

I waved my hands over my head as the headlights came closer. Thank goodness. I was saved. For a car that had been chasing storms, there was a surprising lack of equipment attached to it. When the driver exited the car, I knew I had just made a deadly mistake.

Lonnie Carello came over and took me by the arm.

"Are you okay?"

"I think I need to go to the hospital, or even the shelter."

"Well of course. I'll be glad to drive you there. What in the world are you doing out here all by yourself?"

I realized I hadn't taken the time to dig the extra flares out of the closet. My whole reason for being here was now a lie.

"My husband told me to meet him here," I said as Lonnie helped me into the car. He reached out to me, and I was sure he was about to snap my neck. I flinched and then he handed me the seatbelt.

"We need to be safe, especially now, little mama. I'm quite surprised your husband left you out in the storm. I certainly wouldn't let my pregnant wife alone for a minute. Hey, I heard the funniest thing about you. Someone said you had a knack for solving murders. I had no idea you were so talented. Any ideas on our horse thief?"

"My husband is with the storm chasers, and he told me he could just pick me up on the way. You know, I think I should probably just wait for him. He'll be so upset if he doesn't find me here. Maybe the storm slowed them down. You know, as a matter of fact, I think I'll just wait here for him."

"I can't let you do that sweetie. You could going into labor right here, and you would be all by yourself. No. Papa Lonnie is going to take care of you tonight." He closed my door with a resounding click and headed for his side.

I could just open the door and jump out. Would he drag me back? What kind of danger would it put me and the baby in? What kind of danger were we in already? My mind was racing, and as he got into the car I tried to open my door to get out.

"No really. I'll just wait for my husband." Lonnie Carello put a hand on my other arm, squeezing just a little too tightly.

"I can't believe you're refusing a ride from me. I won't hear another word. I couldn't face myself if you got in trouble out here in the storm by yourself. Now let go of the door." His last few words were no longer laced with the artificial friendliness he was so full of when he first found me. I shut the car door and he hit the gas. I shot up a prayer as another contraction began. *Let Leo find me.*

CHAPTER 23

I pulled my phone out of my pocket. "I'll just text my family and let them know I'm on the way."

The bars I'd proudly displayed to my family earlier were now flat. The storm must have knocked out the cell tower. And my ability to call for help.

"No coverage. I promised my family I wouldn't be long."

"So what were you doing at the police station all alone?" Lonnie asked.

"I was checking on something."

"Go on..."

I didn't answer, and hoped he would let it drop. No way could I tell him I had been at the police station digging through the innards of a cow—*his* cow, which just happened to be stuffed full of neatly wrapped bills.

Lonnie kept his eyes on the road. My heart was pounding so hard against my ribs, I wondered if he could hear it. Probably not, since the wind outside was getting louder by the minute. I looked up just as a plastic grocery bag collided with a swaying stoplight, wrapping around it like a bandage. My labor pains seemed to be mimicking the wind gusts. I crossed my arms over my middle.

"Looks like it won't be too long now," Lonnie said.

When I regained my breath I answered. "Yes. Were you headed to the shelter?"

"... Sure," he answered.

I knew Lonnie Carello hadn't been driving to the shelter when he spotted me. Given the direction he was headed, he may have been coming *from* the shelter, but he certainly wasn't going *toward* it. He was about to break into the police station, but before he could, he found me standing in front. I suspected he was lying, but wasn't sure what he suspected of me.

"You know the shelter was back there," I said, pointing behind me. I hoped Carello was so new to Pecan Bayou he didn't realize his mistake.

"Was it? I just thought we would take a little shortcut." I don't know what kind of shortcut he thought he was taking, but I thought it was a bad idea, since we were driving directly through the wind and rain.

I tried to remain calm. If I couldn't be calm, I had to at least sound calm in order to think my way out of this. I was escaping for two this time around.

"Just what brought you to Pecan Bayou, anyway?" I asked, trying to sound friendly.

The wind whipped more debris across our path. Before Lonnie could answer my question, a large pine tree uprooted and crashed onto the roof of a house.

"Damn," Carello swore. "That was close."

I desperately wished it had landed across the road because then I could have scrambled out of the car.

"Pardon my French," he apologized. "You Texans sure know how to have a storm."

"So where are you from originally?" I asked, still trying to sound normal, not terrified.

"Chicago."

"That explains the accent. You took over Cattleman's Call a few months ago when Mr. Neuwitt retired. Where did he retire to? I don't believe I ever heard. Strange how he was here, then just up and left. So what led you to buy a business here in a small town like Pecan Bayou?"

Lonnie swerved to avoid a flying trash can lid .

"Don't really know where Ron went. Why Pecan Bayou, you ask? Well, I guess you could say I was a silent partner in the business for years. I decided to retire away from Chicago winters, and Texas seemed like a good option. Nice warm weather in these parts. Ron was ... well, let's say, easily convinced to let me take over the business. He was ready for something different as well."

"I see. You sure have been doing a lot of remodeling."

"Yeah." His eyes scanned the road as he navigated through the storm. "Ron let the place go to hell. Beams were rotting, and it needed a lot of repairs just to get it up to code."

"Cattleman's Call wasn't up to code?"

I found this surprising, since if a restaurant in town wasn't up to code, Rocky would be sure to report it in the Gazette. One of Rocky's heroes was Marvin Zindler, an iconic Houston reporter famous for his regular restaurant reports on the evening news. Rocky drew inspiration from Marvin Zindler and would type up his weekly health department report chanting Marvin's signature line *Slime in the ice machiiiiine.* Oh how I longed for Rocky's annoying little chant right now.

If Cattleman's Call had code violations, everybody would've known it. It was one of the nicer eating establishments in town. Lonnie Carello hadn't been remodeling, but searching. Searching for whatever it was hidden inside that cow.

Lonnie interrupted my thoughts. "So what were you doing at the police station to begin with? Seems strange to find you there all alone. There weren't even any police at the station. Do you have a key to the building?"

"Why would you think that?"

"Come on Betsy. You're the daughter of the head honcho cop over there. I can't imagine you would want to be hanging around outside for no reason, so you had to be doing something inside. I'm guessing you have your own key but I'm curious as to what you needed it for.."

Lonnie Carello knew I had a key. He also now knew he could get into the police department without even breaking a window to do it. As we came up to the next stoplight he turned to the left. As much as I hoped he had decided to drive to the shelter, I knew exactly where we were heading.

"Why are we going back?"

Carello did not respond to my question. He focused forward with steely determination. His pleasant demeanor had now slipped for good. I repeated my question.

"I said, why are we turning back?"

"I think you know."

"No. I don't know. Tell me about it." The baby pushed down again, harder this time. I leaned over in pain. Lonnie drove on, ignoring my obvious discomfort.

"Listen, I don't know what's going on, but I need to get to the hospital. I'm in labor."

"Yeah, well, pretty inconvenient for you, if you ask me. I got more important things on my mind. Listen, women drop those things all the time. You'll be fine. Now, shut your face and quit complaining."

I had to get out of this car. We couldn't be going more than five to ten miles an hour, given the force of the wind. I glanced at the speedometer.

"What are you doing?" he said, following my gaze.

"What do you mean?"

"Enough of this, and don't even think about trying to jump out. You want to save that baby, you'd better sit tight."

"Fine." I pulled my hand off the door, and laid it across my belly. "Seeing as you now have decided your trip to the police station is more important than my safe delivery, the least you can do is tell me who you really are. What is it you want in the police station? What was it you were looking for at Cattleman's Call?"

Lonnie smiled.

"You're smarter than you look, Miss Hinter lady. You really wanna know what I was looking for? Fair enough. Maybe, just maybe, there was some money hidden somewhere. Maybe, just maybe, two guys who were best friends robbed a check cashing store in 1978. Maybe one guy went to prison for it and the other guy didn't. One guy kept the money and thought he could get away with it. That thief Neuwitt always told me he had my stake hidden somewhere. When I got out of prison, I came to collect and he got all whiny, saying the money was dirty. He had started a new life in a piss-ant of a town. He told me he was saving me by withholding my share of the money. Said I'd never find it, and I should go start my own life doing good in the world. What a load of crap. So one thing led to another, you might say."

"Meaning you killed Ron Neuwitt?"

"What? Are you wearing a wire or something?"

"Hardly." Even if I were, who could be hearing me in this storm? Lonnie's eyes narrowed, and he continued.

"Why no, sweetheart. Let's just say he disappeared, and they won't find him for years. Maybe he went off to start another new life doing good."

Another pine tree fell, this time landing in the road. Lonnie Carello swerved around it, barely avoiding impact. My body slammed against the door, and as it did, another contraction hit. I bent over using my Lamaze breathing, trying to work through it until it passed.

"Oh yeah, that kid is coming. I've been in the delivery room. This is where there ain't no turning back. Too bad I have to be here with you. Last time it was excruciating to watch. Especially seeing as they won't let you smoke in there. Buck up sweetie, you're not going to get any help from a doctor."

"Listen to yourself. This isn't right, and you know it."

He pulled into a parking space in front of the Pecan Bayou police station. "Yeah well nothing I can do about it now. Hand me the key, Mama."

I reached into my purse and pulled out the single key my father had given me attached to a police department key fob. I thought for a moment maybe I would give him the wrong key to stall for time.

"Give me the key. Don't try to pull anything. Oh, and give me your cell phone."

I searched in my purse trying to cover my cell phone with my hand.

"It's not here. I must have dropped it under the seat." I tried to pretend searching beneath the seat, but the bulk of the baby kept me from reaching the floor.

Lonnie grabbed the purse out of my hands. "I told you not to try anything." He reached in my purse and pulled out my cell phone. Holding it up he said, "How stupid do you think I am? A pregnant woman without a working cell phone? I'm not playing here. I'm not one of these local yokel yahoos here. In Chicago we're a little brighter than that."

I wished he would go back to Chicago. I liked the yahoos here much better. As he exited the car he leaned down and said, "You stay here. Normally I'd take you with me, but in your condition you ain't going nowhere. Maybe you could have the kid before I come back? Oh, and don't get any blood on the seats."

"You can't just leave me here," I said, breathing through another contraction.

"Yes I can." He sneered.

He opened the door to the police station with my key and ran inside. As the contraction eased, I tried to come up with a new plan. A little puddle dripped down onto the floorboard as I felt my water breaking. I hoped I ruined his upholstery.

I pulled myself out of the car, struggling with the door. The wind kicked up a newspaper that slapped against my leg. If I could just avoid being hit by storm debris, maybe I could make it to the shelter. Nolan Ryan Middle school was about four blocks away and then I just had to cross the bridge. That would be the toughest part because there would be no buildings to protect me, and a heavy wind could pitch me into the water if I didn't get to the guardrail soon enough.

I started walking, staying as close as possible to the sides of the buildings in downtown Pecan Bayou. About every ten feet or so another contraction would hit. I would stop, lean against the wall and breathe through it. I had to do this. I had to make it for me and Leo and our baby.

Walking was the worst thing to be doing right now since it speeds up delivery, but it was the best thing for me to do given the situation. It was my only way out.

I thought about what Lonnie Carello said about women who dropped babies in the middle of work. I wasn't that girl. I was the one who asked for extra epidural juice, chipped ice and pleasant music in the background. For just a moment, I thought of the birthing suite Leo and I had signed up for three months ago. Our little hospital tried to replicate the birthing suites in the big cities. There wasn't a birthing tub, or a specialty birthing chair, but they did have a big screen TV, a bubba recliner and a mini fridge that would hold enough Lone Star beer to get any couple through an average length delivery.

No luxurious surroundings for this baby to come into, unfortunately. Even if I did get the baby suite, I didn't have a doctor to deliver me. None of that mattered unless I got away from Lonnie Carello.

If he hadn't been so anxious to get his hands on the money, he probably would have killed me while he had me in the car. Killing a mother and her child wouldn't faze him. He had already killed two people trying to recover his stolen cash.

I kept moving, desperate to get far enough away he wouldn't be able to hunt me down. I saw car lights coming toward me. Carello must have found the money by now and was going to take care of me next.

I slid into a doorway and held myself tightly against the door as a tremor worked its way through me. All I could do was hope he hadn't seen me. The car inched closer, and then slowed down in the park right in front of me. Nothing like trying to hide an elephant behind a skinny tree.

"Betsy?"

The voice was so familiar, I gasped. With the wind I couldn't be sure.

"Betsy? Is that you?"

I didn't know what to do. If that was Carello, he would kill me. If it was somebody who could save me, I could miss the chance of a rescue by staying hidden.

The words of my last dream echoed in my ears.

"Betsy step into the wind. It'll only do you good."

I stepped out from the doorway. Standing in front of a white, storm-battered minivan with the words "Storm Chasers" painted in bold red letters, stood the love of my life, Leo Fitzpatrick.

"Leo!" I ran into his arms and felt his strong arms encircle me. I had found home in the middle of a tempest.

"Betsy! What the hell are you doing out here? You have to be the craziest woman on the planet, you know that?" he scolded.

"Lonnie Carello..." As I started to explain, another contraction hit me. I stopped and bent over, his arms still holding me up.

"That's right. Breathe, Betsy, breathe." As it passed, I took a deep breath and then tried to finish my story. "Lonnie Carello. He killed Connor Holman. We have to get out of here."

One of the storm chasers came out of the van and around to my other side.

"Leo, is she going into labor? Is she going to have the baby?"

Just like watching a tornado, the guy was documenting my behavior. "I'm right here."

"Oh. Nate Collins, this is my wife Betsy. Betsy, this is the guy I've been telling you about."

"Nice to meet you," Nate said. "Wow! What an exciting day. First, we get a tornado on tape and now we're going to have a baby."

Nate turned toward the van. "Hey guys, come out here a minute." A ragtag crew piled out of the back of the van. Three more men and one petite woman now stood around me. Nate put his hand on my shoulder as if showing his staff a weather pattern on a map.

"Leo's wife, here is in labor. We have to get her to the hospital." As he spoke the wooden pig that hung in front of with Benny's barbecue went flying past us. Why not? All the other fake animals were loose.

"No way that's going to happen. The road to the hospital washed out an hour ago. We barely made it into town. If the bridge to the middle school is still intact, we can make it over there," Nate said.

I couldn't wait any longer. I placed my hand on Leo's arm to pull him out of the planning session. "We have to go."

"Okay. There's not a lot of room in the van, but we can sit on each other's laps." Nate said.

"We have to go," I said again as another contraction hit me.

"Don't worry Bets, we're going."

"No. Lonnie Carello. If he finds me, he'll kill me."

"Why would Lonnie Carello kill you?" Leo asked.

"Because I know about the money. He had money hidden in the cow."

"Is this labor dementia?" One of the chasers from the back seat chimed in. "Dude. I saw this once on YouTube." Obviously, I was in a car full of bachelors.

"Shut up. She's saying something important," said the woman, who was now sitting on the lap of a man with a bushy beard and a t-shirt that read *I brake for tornadoes*.

A set of car lights glared in the rear view mirror.

"That's him," I said. "We have to get away."

Nate squinted his eyes as he looked into the oncoming light.

"Love to, but this idiot is right behind me, and we are in the middle of a high gust pattern." Nate swerved to the side of the road and stopped to avoid a flying trash can. It clanked down the street in front of us.

"We have to..." Before I could finish my sentence another contraction hit.

"Have you been timing these contractions?" Leo asked.

"Sort of. I lost track when the whole *I'll kill you* thing came up."

The car behind us had stopped, and Lonnie Carello was now walking toward our vehicle.

"Jesus, we're in trouble," piped up one of the backseat passengers.

"Shut up, you idiot," the woman whispered.

"It's Lonnie Carello," I said. "He killed Connor Holman."

Carello tapped on the glass.

"Everybody, just act like we're in a hurry to get Betsy to the hospital. Stay calm."

Leo unrolled his window.

"Well, there you are Betsy," Carello said. "I was getting worried about you."

"Yes. I told you my husband would be here."

"You sure did. I guess I should've believed you. I think we still have some things we need to talk about, though. Why don't you just get on out of the car, and I won't be forced to do anything to anybody else. You get my drift?"

"She's not getting out of the car," Leo said.

Lonnie Carello pulled out a gun. "Yeah? I think you're wrong about that."

"What are you going to do? Shoot all of us?"

"If I have to. This isn't my first rodeo. Isn't that what you cowboys like to say?"

Nate leaned over Leo. "Yeah. And you're not the first demon of a storm we've come up against in this car." He yanked the car into reverse, ramming the front of Lonnie Carello's car, and jumping the curb, sped forward, putting Carello behind us.

"Oh my God. You got away." I was amazed how well Nate maneuvered the van.

A bullet whizzed past the window and shattered the passenger side mirror.

"Everybody get down," Nate yelled.

As much as I wanted to comply, there was no way I could scrunch down. I saw the rough chain link fence from the police impound yard sail in front of us. A single headlight was now gaining behind us. Lonnie Carello intended to chase us down. It was insane, but then again so was he.

As we approached the bridge, Carello started ramming the van. He was clearly trying to drive us off the road into the Bayou. If it looked like we were killed in the storm, his problems would be solved.

"Hold on everybody," Nate said.

All of the animals stored in the impound yard were now twisting around in the wind. Connor Holman's menagerie was airborne. He would have been so inspired to see them all. As they started into a downward spiral, we dodged the flying chicken, and the cow from Cattleman's Call clanked across the top of the van. As we made our way onto the bridge, the cow flew straight into Lonnie Carello's car. As he swerved to avoid it, his car flew over the bank and down into the waters of Pecan Bayou.

CHAPTER 24

"Should we go back and get him?"

"No," Leo said. "That's what the police are for. We don't have time to be fishing some mobster out of the bayou. Did you forget we're having a baby here?"

When we entered the shelter, we found most of the population of Pecan Bayou now huddled around camping lanterns and candles. The storm had finally taken the power out. Benny's Barbecue and Birdie's Diner had each set up tables, getting rid of food that would have spoiled if left unrefrigerated. Maggie, who was sitting next to Danny on a cot, rushed over and took me by the elbow.

"Lord a mighty, Betsy. You sure put me through it tonight. I can't believe you went out in that storm alone." I bent over for a contraction.

"Oh my land. She's having the baby." Maggie turned from us and shot her hand up in the air making a circular motion.

"Attention everybody! We have a baby coming. We need anybody who can help us to get over here right away."

"Do we have anyone with medical training? " Mayor Obermeyer shouted from his lawn chair. Baxter Digby was next to him, his eyes focused across the gym on Sasha Holman.

"Is Dr. Randall here?" Leo said.

"I'm here if you need me, Betsy." Ruby Green's bracelets clanked in my ear.

"I've delivered a foal before if that's any help," Libby Loper said as she got up and crossed the room. There was so much chatter going on I thought my head would split.

"Take my pillow Betsy. It has sweet dreams on it, "Danny said, handing me his treasured possession.

My eyes filled as I spoke. "Thank you, Danny. I'll take good care of it."

"I know you will." He nodded and backed up.

"We're going to need something to give her some privacy," Libby said.

"We need to keep her in the gym. It's still the safest place in the school." Mayor Obermeyer said.

Phylliss Hamlin, head of the PTA stepped up. "We can drag some of our portable room dividers to the corner to give Betsy some privacy. That's the best we can do."

"Sounds good. Let's go people," Aunt Maggie said. "Can somebody round us up some sort of a bed or a couch?"

"There's one in the nurse's office. Tyler and I can get it." I had seen that thing once or twice. It was more of a vinyl table, but it was better than the floor.

"Good," Aunt Maggie said as she led me across the gym towards the corner to sit in a folding chair until the bed arrived.

"Do we have any doctors here? We'll even take a veterinarian," Maggie said.

An attractive well-dressed woman walked over. She looked familiar to me, but I couldn't place her. I had seen her somewhere. She ran her finger behind her ear pushing back a straight piece of black hair.

"I'm a midwife. Does that count? I've never delivered a foal, but I do have some experience with people. It's been years, but I think I can remember what to do."

I reached out and squeezed her hand. "It counts," I said through a cleansing breath. Leo leaned into the teeming group of women around me.

"What do we need to do?" he asked.

"Okay," the woman said, "you need some scissors, towels and disinfectant. We'll need something to wrap the baby in once he arrives."

People ran off in all directions to their appointed tasks. The room dividers were brought in and put around us. They were still partially open for the people that would be bringing in necessary supplies.

The door of the gym clanged behind us. My father removed his Stetson, shaking off the water. Behind him was Elaina, in a bright yellow rain slicker. As soon as he saw the crowd gathered around me he whooped, "Are you having the baby?"

Before I could answer a hard contraction hit me. He ran to my side.

"I just got finished going up and down the roads making sure everybody was safe. I'm here now darlin'."

"You're going to have to go out again," I gasped.

"No, I'm not. Everyone's here."

"Yes, you are. I know who murdered Connor Holman."

"Really? Now Betsy? I think you have a hell of a lot more important things to think about at this moment."

"No, it's Lonnie Carello... He's... in the bayou..."

"What is she talking about?" My father scanned the group that had gathered in the corner next to the room dividers.

"It's true, dude," said the bearded storm chaser. "He followed us here and shot at us and everything."

"Is everybody okay? Was anyone hit? "

"No one was hit. The van took a couple of bullets. We left Carello in the Bayou," Nate said.

"Out there in the storm? I'll be damned."

"He was shooting at us. When we found Betsy, she kept saying he was the killer. I know it all sounds crazy, but it has something to do with the cow," Leo said, shaking his head in confusion.

A look of recognition came across my father's face. "The cow at the station?"

"Yes," I answered, out of breath. "Carello might be dying. He swerved off into the bayou." My father put his hat put back on. "Sometimes I hate this job. I'll go get this fool, but I'm depending on everybody here to take good care of my daughter. My grandchild is coming into the world, and we need to do it right."

Elaina came back from the mobile station Mrs. Thatcher had set up in the corner. "I tried to get Orley. He's out with the crew rescuing old man Jennings."

Drummond Struthers seemed to appear out of nowhere. "Judd, you can't go out there alone. Let me go with you."

"I can't ask you to do that. It could be dangerous."

"Not as dangerous as it would be if you were alone. I know you have your hands full with this storm, and I parked the tow truck outside in case we would need it later."

"You're a good man, Drum. Normally, I wouldn't let you come with me, but tonight I'd appreciate the help." Drummond Struthers stepped back, kissed his wife goodbye and followed my dad. Baxter Digby busied himself trying to open a water bottle.

Zach and Tyler rushed across the gym wobbling along with the nurse's office cot. Once they had it in place behind the dividers, Zach took the hand of a woman I vaguely recognized. "Mom, I brought Mrs. Powell. She's our school nurse. She can deliver your baby."

"Oh my." She put her hand to her throat. "I put on Band-aids and check for fevers. When you told me you wanted me to meet your mother, I had no idea you needed me to deliver her baby."

"It's okay. Really," I said between breaths.

"I'll be glad to assist in any way I can, but you're pretty far out of my league."

"Great," said the midwife, turning to Mrs. Powell. "I'll deliver and you assist."

I looked at my rescuer. Why was she so familiar? Where had I seen her?

She noticed me staring at her. "Tell me what you're feeling, Betsy."

"I'm sorry. Have we met before?"

"I don't know. Have you ever bought a house from my husband?"

"Your husband?"

"Yes. He's right over..." She paused as she searched the gym. Finally, she pointed to Baxter Digby who was having a heated conversation with Sasha Holman. My guess was that Sasha had finally told Digby about Rocky's upcoming article covering their affair. "...there." She scowled.

"Isn't your husband running for city council?" The school nurse's eyes now cast downward. She knew too. I could tell.

"That's what he's telling people," Mrs. Digby replied.

"Then he should be a natural," the nurse said, not realizing the slight.

I debated telling her about what I knew about her husband, but suspected she already knew.

"Sure," Mrs. Digby said. "I just wonder what the voters of the good town of Pecan Bayou would think about a guy who cheats on his wife? Does it shock you I said that? I mean I'm pretty sure the whole town knows about it. They haven't exactly been discreet. Don't worry about me. I'll get him in the divorce settlement. He'll be sorry he ever messed with me. By the way, it's nice to meet you. I'm Dana."

"I think he's lost my vote," I said.

"Mine too," nodded Mrs. Powell.

"Never had mine to begin with," Maggie added.

Another contraction hit me hard. Aunt Maggie, seeing the fear in my eyes, placed her hand over mine. I had planned on having this baby in the hospital, with a doctor and a plethora of pain killers. I didn't plan on having it in what was the equivalent of a town fair.

"This is my fault. If I hadn't been so stupid about that cow, I could have parked myself at the hospital before the road washed out." Tears were running down my face.

"Betsy, look at me." Maggie stared at me, and I was pulled back to reality. My aunt's eyes looked large in her thick glasses. Her warmth and steady touch calmed me. "It's going to be all right. Women have been having babies for thousands of years. You'll be fine."

She looked up at Leo who was now wearing out a patch of the beautiful new rubberized floor of the gym. "You're going to survive too, Leo. Just land somewhere, okay?"

There was a knocking on the divider and Leo stuck his head out. Nate stepped forward. "We need to be on our way now, Leo. We're going to try and head out on the other side of town. There's funnel clouds still out there. Let us know if it's a boy or a girl."

"Will do, and thanks for letting me ride along."

"And thanks for getting us in a shootout," said the storm chaser chick. "As if these testosterone-fueled guys didn't have enough adrenalin rushes going on." Leo bid goodbye to the storm chasers and pulled the dividers back together. He came over to me and took my hand in his holding it securely and somehow making the pain go away, just for a second.

I was taking a breath between contractions. They were coming hard and fast now. I looked over at Dana Digby. "When I visited your husband's office, I saw a photograph in the reception area with you standing next to him."

"Yeah, well treasure it. We won't be taking too many group shots in the future. I'm filing for divorce."

Another contraction hit. Leo stood guard at the opening making sure we had privacy.

"Okay," Dana said, as she looked under the blanket that was hastily draped over my legs. "Looks like we're having ourselves a baby."

The school nurse handed Dana a pair of rubber gloves which she quickly slipped onto her hands.

"The baby is starting to crown. Here comes a contraction. Maggie, Mrs. Powell, lift her legs up, and Betsy put your chin down on your chest and focus all your energy on pushing the baby out."

Dana Digby started counting to ten while I pushed through the pain. At the end of the contraction, I regained my breath.

"You're doing great. It won't be long now."

"For a woman out of practice, you seem to know what you're doing," I told her.

"Thanks, but it isn't over yet. Baxter wanted me to stay at home with the children and really, so did I. Now, the kids are getting older and with everything thing else that's been going on, I'd been thinking about getting back to work lately, anyway."

Her appearance had saved me, and I felt beholden to her.

A contraction hit me again and we resumed our efforts.

Dana looked down again. "Okay, now push."

I pushed as hard as I could, feeling the baby coming down the birth canal. I thought it would hurt more without pain killers, but instead I had the strength to get through without anything. I had just escaped a killer. This was as easy as pie.

A few minutes later a beautiful baby girl became the newest member of the town of Pecan Bayou. Mrs. Powell and Dana Digby did their best to clean her up and when she let out a healthy wail in protest, the chatter in the gymnasium stopped.

Mrs. Powell stepped out of our makeshift delivery room with the baby, wrapped in a towel. "It's a girl!"

She handed the baby to Leo, who held her like a precious piece of porcelain.

He looked down at his precious daughter and then made his way over to me. His blue eyes rimmed with tears.

Once I was covered up, Aunt Maggie opened up the dividers. "Well, Mrs. Fitzpatrick. Aren't you full of surprises? I thought we had a boy."

As if sensing her audience, the baby cried out once again, her voice loud and strong. Danny, Tyler, and Zach came running over and surrounded us.

"The baby is here! The baby is here!" Danny said, jumping up and down while holding Zach's hands. I felt Leo's strong grip on my shoulder.

"She's beautiful. We made ourselves an incredible little human being."

"The direct result of true love," Aunt Maggie whispered through tears.

He bent down and kissed me on the forehead, then kissed his daughter. Our little girl stopped crying for just a moment as her large blue eyes stared at Leo.

"She's a beautiful baby," said Leo's mother. "I can't believe you delivered her through all of this."

As I pulled her close to me I noticed the color of her hair. It was a deep rich brown.

Leo reached down and ran his fingers through her silken hair. "You know, I have to say her hair is the same color as the cocoa pecan pie at Benny's Barbecue. Do you think so?"

Benny and Celia stepped forward from the crowd, and then Benny slapped at his knee.

"I'll be darned. It is the same color as my pie. You got yourself a sweet little miss there, Betsy. I told you it was special cocoa that made it so good."

He was right. It was the same color. If anybody was really noticing though, it was also the color of my own hair. As if she knew we were talking about her, the baby cried once again. I looked up at Dana Digby and took her hand. "I can't thank you enough for all you've done tonight."

"I'm just so glad I was here and able to help. Sometimes it feels good to be more than the wife of Baxter Digby."

"You are so much more," I told her.

"Betsy. Smile for the camera." A light flashed in my face as Rocky took my picture.

There are times in a woman's life when she doesn't want her picture taken. The first few minutes after giving birth ranks pretty high on the list. I knew I would be featured in a special storm issue of the Gazette. Lucky me. Rocky put his camera down and came over and took a close up of my daughter.

"I thought you'd be off getting pictures of my dad fishing out Carello" I said.

"Ah, I let Nicholas take that one. Wouldn't look right for me to get all the big stories. It's important for a parent to let his child shine now and again." Rocky looked down at the baby. "She's a keeper. What are you calling her? I'll need to put it in the paper."

I didn't know what to tell him. I guess in the back of my mind all along I had thought it was another boy. It was so wonderful to be holding this little girl in my arms, I felt tears coming down.

"Oh, that's all right darlin'. You can tell me later," Rocky said.

My voice was so full of emotion, I almost didn't get my answer out. "Coco?"

"Coco," Leo said. He thought about it. "I like it. But I would like to add the middle name." He reached over and took Aunt Maggie's hand. "Let's call her Coco Margaret Fitzpatrick."

"Perfect," I whispered.

CHAPTER 25

"Ain't that sweet. You had your kid."

Lonnie Carello, drenched and panting, stood in the crowd. He ran his fingers through his wet black hair, slicking it back and making him look like a gangster. A plastic grocery bag stuffed full of cash dangled from his arm, and in his hand was a gun.

He had clearly slipped into the gym unnoticed during all the excitement. Two dark eyes set in a haggard face met mine.

"That's him. That's who killed Connor Holman," I said.

"Yeah well I'm old news, right sweetheart?" He turned and pointed the gun at the crowd.

"All I need is some keys, and I'll leave you townsfolk alone. Who's going to be smart here and hand me their keys? Give me a way out of here, and no one gets killed. What you say we start the hair lady here?" He grabbed the back of Ruby's neck, pulling her in front of him.

"Where's my father?" I demanded.

"I guess that's for me to know and you to find out."

"Listen up mister." Baxter Digby, sensing his chance to gain the crowd's approval, stepped forward, adjusting the sleeves of his blazer. He might have been threatening and controlling towards the women in his life, but I doubted he would fare so well taking on a guy like Carello. Nevertheless, he continued.

"You can see this is a gathering of the good people of Pecan Bayou. I don't know what your business is, but I think you need to go back out into the storm." He fished in his pocket. "Take my keys. It's the silver Escalade by the light pole."

"That's mighty kind of you, pardner." He grabbed the keys and gestured to Benny with his gun. "You, put some of that grub into a box for me."

Benny quickly complied shoving barbecue into a styrofoam container.

"When you're finished with the car, I would appreciate it if you would leave it somewhere safe and call me," Baxter added.

"Are you kidding me?" Carello responded. "Do you want me to shoot you right now?" Baxter's hands went up to his most precious commodity, his face.

"Better yet, keep it," he said from behind his hands.

Lonnie Carello laughed as he backed up to the beverage table, pouring himself a cup of coffee while holding a steady gun on the crowd. Nothing like a caffeinated killer to get you through the night.

"Everybody sit down, mind your own business and nobody gets hurt. I'm only here to get a car and blow this town. After tonight, I'll just be a bad memory, like my time in this two stoplight town." He guzzled down his coffee, squeezed the styrofoam cup into a pulpy mess, and threw it on the floor.

The people in the shelter stood frozen in tableau. It was pretty hard to turn their backs on a confessed killer. Leo, in an attempt to protect his family, gathered Zach and Tyler closer to him.

Aunt Maggie screamed. "Danny! Danny's gone." He had been standing off to the side next to the boys. When had he disappeared? Could he have gone out in the storm?

"He has to be here somewhere," Birdie said. "Danny?" She called out.

Much to Lonnie Carello's delight, the town of Pecan Bayou was now following his directions. They were ignoring him. He grinned and crossed his arms as he watched the mayhem of the search.

Just as he was about to start walking for the door with Ruby, he was hit on the head. Ruby scooted out of the way, bracelets clanking, as Rocky and Benny jumped on Carello, knocking him to the door.

Mayor Obermeyer stood behind the men with his precious artifact, the remnant of the first pecan tree planted in Pecan Bayou, now broken into two pieces.

"Oh my gosh, Mayor! The log is ruined." Ruby said.

"It's just an old piece of wood. We're safe, and somehow I think my great-great grandfather Tobias would have approved."

"Man, Rocky, looks like you're going have to write about yourself in your own newspaper," Benny said, as he tied up Lonnie Carello's hands with a crocheted shawl from one of the women in the crowd.

"Yeah, I like to report the news, but not necessarily be in it."

Baxter Digby stood safely within the crowd. He reached for his wife's hand only to be pushed away.

"Okay, people," Maggie said. "The excitement is over. Now we have some of our people missing here. Let's get out there and find them."

She turned towards me. "You keep that baby warm."

She leaned down and kissed my daughter. "Welcome to the world, Coco Pop. Now your great-auntie is going to round up the rest of your crazy family"

"Why don't I come with you? Betsy has plenty of people to watch after her here," Leo offered.

Maggie smiled appreciatively. "Are you sure?"

"It's just bad weather. After a couple of hours with the storm chasers, I think I can handle it."

Leo grabbed his coat and then took Tyler and Zach aside. "Look after your mother and your ... sister."

The door to the gym slammed shut. Judd, whose glasses were now broken and hanging by a thread, came through the door with Danny, who was holding a drenched box that had, at one time, had a hand painted wrapper on it.

"Look who I found out in the storm," my father said, taking off his glasses and rubbing his eyes.

Maggie ran over and put her arms around a dripping Danny.

"I had to give the baby her gift. It was just at the day-hab," Danny said. Danny's day-habilitation center was only a block away.

"I know, baby, but it was dangerous. You shouldn't have done that without telling Mama. How did you get in?"

"The door." He looked her as if she was being silly. "It was swinging in the wind. I had to give the baby her gift," he repeated.

"I know it was important to you."

"It got wet."

"That's okay. I don't think she'll mind."

"I made it for her. It got wet."

"Well, then let's take it to her."

Danny pulled a clumsily hand-sewn felt doll out of the box. "For you, baby."

Of all the baby gifts we had received, this little item had to be the least attractive. Rough workmanship aside, my daughter's deep blue eyes latched onto it as her head turned toward the raggedy doll.

"She likes it," Danny said.

"Of course, she does. She's going to like you even more."

"I love her, Betsy."

I survived a killer, a tornado and a flying cow, but at this moment, I felt at peace. I set the little doll next to Coco and snuggled close to her tiny form. I could really use a nap about now.

CHAPTER 26

"Mr. and Mrs. Fitzpatrick, I've brought you your baby." The nurse gently lowered Coco into my arms. It seemed strange to have the baby taken away once we arrived at the hospital, but of course she had to be properly checked out by the medical staff after being born outside the wonders of modern medicine.

"She's as fit as a fiddle," Dr. Randall said, as she entered the room holding a clipboard. "Here, we rely on high-tech instruments, and you did it all with a gym towel and a football jersey."

"Not true. I had an amazing midwife helping me through it."

"Yes, I heard that. We need to get this woman on staff here."

"She just might be looking for a job," I said, thinking Baxter Digby would be served with his divorce papers any day now.

"We couldn't have made it through without her," Leo said. I handed the baby to him. He gathered Coco up and did a little dance around the room. He was so sweet when he was goofy.

A giant teddy bear appeared at the door. My father's head peeked out over the bear's shoulder.

"How is my granddaughter?"

"Oh, Dad. You know the baby has a mountain of gifts already. I think everyone in town has given her something. After all this, we won't have any room left in the nursery for the baby."

"Well then, you'll just have to start putting stuff in the den because this grandpa is not done giving his precious angel anything she wants."

"You'll spoil her."

"Just like I did you," he said.

"I think you did an excellent job," Leo said.

"And I thank you for that."

Leo's mother Gwyn rose from the recliner and tried to place the bear on the window sill next to another much smaller bear. "Trying to outdo me, Judd? Now my little bear looks terrible next to yours."

"It's great you brought these things," I said, "but I think Coco loves Danny's gift the best." In the layette was the hand-pieced doll Danny had brought her in the storm.

"You just might be right there," my father said. "There's nothing like homemade to outclass store bought any day. Oh and by the way, Rocky says he wants an interview on your perilous ride with the killer while in labor."

"I'm sure he does."

"I'll be glad to get your side of the story too, because Carello has lawyered up. What did he tell you?"

"He said the money hidden inside the cow was from the robbery of a check cashing store back in 1978."

"We knew that from Carello's record. They caught him on camera back then, but he never gave up the name of his partner. We now know it was Ron Neuwitt. Good old Ron. If you had asked me who was behind a strong arm robbery in this town, I never would have come up with Neuwitt. Everybody loved that guy. You just never know. Mr. Neuwitt took the money and hid it, while Carello served the time."

"So that was what all the construction was for? He was looking for the hidden cash?" Leo asked.

"Yes. The thing was, I think Ron Neuwitt changed after he came to Pecan Bayou. I don't know if it was the fresh air or the people here, but he spent very little of the money. He met and married his wife here, raised kids and left his life of crime behind him. I'll bet most of the money is still there. He stuffed it inside the cow, and didn't spend it."

"Well, we do have Carello's prison record, so though he's hiding behind his lawyer, we do have him holding the stolen money from the original crime. Now, we just have to put him at the death of Connor Holman and connect him to Neuwitt's disappearance. I'm figuring

Holman had no idea there was money hidden inside his precious stolen cow, but he was the only thing between Carello and the money. He killed him but before he could grab the cash, you and Rocky showed up. You had a way of getting yourself in the middle of this guy's plans."

"Yes. I have to tell you I've had my share of adventures, but being in labor and getting in the car with someone I know was a murderer has to be the dumbest thing I've ever done."

"I'll second that," Leo said. Down the hall I could hear the voices of Maggie, Danny, Tyler and Zach.

"Hello baby," Danny said as he entered the room first.

"And how is little Maggie today?" Aunt Maggie followed behind Danny.

"Mama," Danny said, "her name is Coco, not Maggie. That's your name."

"It's her name too. Her middle name. So to you she's Coco, but I think I see a little Maggie." Aunt Maggie held out her arms to Leo, a tear now shining on her cheek. Leo happily obliged and placed Coco in her arms. Coco's tiny hand reached up to Maggie.

"For a child who was born in the school gym, she looks remarkably well."

"Frankly," Gwyn said, "I don't know how you did it. You are a strong woman, Betsy."

"This is going to sound strange, but all along I felt like someone was guiding me. Really, it was several someones."

"Who?" Aunt Maggie asked.

I remembered every message from my dreams, delivered by people in my past: Oliver, Vanessa, Lenny, Hunter, Martha, Eula Jean and Connor. They had all come to me. They were sometimes rude, and sometimes funny, but they each had a message. Had they been real or should I chalk them up to crazy pregnant dreams? I would never know.

"Oh, I don't know. What does it matter now? " I answered.

There was a knock at the door. Benny and Celia stood there with a familiar white bag from Benny's Barbecue.

"Hey there, Betsy. We came by to see the baby," Benny said.

"We knew you wouldn't be able to get in and get your piece of pie so we brought you some." Celia unwrapped the pie and put it before me on the sliding side table.

"You know, I don't want to be ungrateful or anything, but I don't seem to want it. As a matter of fact, the idea of chocolate right now is not sitting well with my stomach."

"Oh man. I knew this would happen. Your cravings have stopped. What am I going to tell the contractor I hired, planning on the extra revenue you generated?" Benny asked.

"Don't worry," Celia said. "I've been running some numbers, and I think we can cut back one waitress." She looked annoyed and then cracked a smile. Benny laughed and put his arm her waist.

It reminded of a time a few years ago when Celia had been pregnant with their daughter, and I envied their affection for each other. I knew, watching them, that they were what true love looked like. My first marriage had been nothing like what I saw between the two of them.

"Betsy?" Leo said, his blue eyes looking lovingly into mine. "I just wanted to say thanks." He kissed me on the forehead. "Thanks for having our baby, and thanks for letting your crazy weather guy run off and chase storms while you were in labor. I'm so glad I knocked you down in that haunted hospital all those years ago. We were like a warm front hitting a cloud formation." He splayed his fingers out and hit his hands together like a cymbal crash. "Boom."

God he was so sexy when he talked weather patterns. That was the moment when I knew my life had come full circle. I had the love of a good husband, family and friends. Life was just what I hoped it would be, living and loving in Pecan Bayou.

HELPFUL HINTS FROM THE HAPPY HINTER

How to Use Epoxy Glue

If you are gluing something together like a broken piggy bank, you need to purchase five-minute epoxy. You may also find a twenty-minute version of the same product, and either will work. This product is a two-part epoxy. It is very messy so put down some paper. Depending how messy you are, you may also want to put on a pair of rubber gloves.

Undo the cap of each tube and press down equal parts of each onto a paper plate. Make sure you have equal amounts of both the yellow and white portions. Take a toothpick and mix the two together, combining them thoroughly.

To apply, get a gob on your toothpick and spread onto the piece you are going to attach to another piece. Position the piece you're gluing and hold it in place until it is glued and stable. Let it set overnight before depositing money back in the bank.

Drummond Struther's Coca-Cola Burgers

1 egg
1/2 cup Coca-Cola, divided
1/2 cup crushed saltine crackers
1/4 cup finely chopped onion
6 tablespoons creamy French dressing, divided
2 Tablespoons grated Parmesan cheese
1/4 teaspoon salt
1 1/2 lbs. lean ground beef
6 hamburger buns, split

In a mixing bowl, combine the egg, 1/4 cup of Coca-Cola, cracker crumbs, onion, 2 tablespoons of the dressing, cheese and salt.

Add the meat and mix well.

Form into six 3/4-inch thick patties.

For the sauce, mix the remaining Coca-Cola and dressing.

Grill the burgers, turning once, basting occasionally with sauce. Serve on buns. Remaining sauce may be used as a topping.

Serves 6.

Birdie's Diner Buttermilk Pecan Chicken

1/2 cup butter
1 cup flour
1 cup ground pecans
1/4 cup sesame seeds
1 tablespoon paprika
1 1/2 teaspoons salt
1/4 teaspoon pepper
1 egg, slightly beaten
1 cup buttermilk
8 boneless chicken breasts
1/4 cup pecans, coarsely chopped

Melt butter in a 9x13 inch baking dish and set aside. Combine flour, ground pecans, sesame seeds, paprika, salt and pepper. Combine egg and buttermilk. Dip chicken in egg mixture then dredge in flour mixture, coating well. Place in baking dish, turning once to coat with butter. Sprinkle with chopped pecans.

Bake chicken at 350 degrees for 30 minutes or until done.

*Make this recipe gluten free by replacing the flour with a gluten-free flour (Bob's Red Mill Gluten Free Flour works well).

Benny's Cocoa Pecan Pie

1 cup sugar

1 cup dark corn syrup

3 large eggs

Dash of salt

2 tablespoons butter, melted

1 1/2 teaspoons vanilla

4 tablespoons cocoa

1 1/2 to 2 cups chopped pecans

1 9-inch unbaked pie shell

Mix sugar, dark corn syrup, eggs, salt, butter, vanilla and cocoa. Add pecans. Pour filling into an unbaked pie shell.

Bake at 375 degrees for 10 minutes; reduce heat to 325 degrees and bake for an additional 40 to 45 minutes or until the filling has solidified.

Baby Shower Games

Baby Name Scramble

At the baby shower, you give each guest a pad of paper and a pen. Have everyone write down the mother's first name and the father's first name. Be sure everyone is spelling these two names correctly. Then, explain that if they scramble the letters from those two names, they can create a list of unique and unusual baby names. If you can't get enough names generated from first names, use middle and last names as well.

Baby Gift Bingo

When your guests arrive with shower gifts, put a number on each box or bag. You should know how many people will be attending so that you can pre-print bingo cards with the correct number of gifts on them. When the mommy-to-be decides to open the presents, she grabs the present she wants to open and reads the number out loud. As soon as someone receives bingo, they win the baby shower game and a baby shower prize, such as a gift basket or gift card.

Pre-Baby Checklist

1. Address your baby announcements. You can put in the details on the birth later.

2. Make sure you are set to go with your medical coverage and that you are signed up at the hospital.

3. Have a pediatrician lined up.

4. Have a car seat and be sure to pack it in the car on the way to the hospital.

5. Stock up on diapers.

6. Make sure your postpartum items are in order, such as feminine napkins and stool softener.

7. Fill the freezer with precooked meals.

8. Make sure you have gas in your car.

9. Do a practice run to the hospital including checking in once you get there.

10. Have your baby bag packed and ready to go!

Don't miss out!

Visit the website below and you can sign up to receive emails whenever Teresa Trent publishes a new book. There's no charge and no obligation.

https://books2read.com/r/B-A-FJQD-HLVP

Did you love *Murder for a Rainy Day*? Then you should read *Oh Holy Fright*[1] by Teresa Trent!

[2]

Read more at https://teresatrent.com.

1. https://books2read.com/u/mVQ2Pr
2. https://books2read.com/u/mVQ2Pr

www.ingramcontent.com/pod-product-compliance
Lightning Source LLC
LaVergne TN
LVHW010617100826
845148LV00014B/3006

* 9 7 8 1 7 3 2 9 4 6 8 5 9 *